BLACK MAGIC RISING

WILDE WITCHES - BOOK 1

ERIN RICHARDS

Midnight Muse
PUBLISHING

BLACK MAGIC RISING
Erin Richards

Print ISBN: 978-1943800162
Digital ISBN: 978-1943800155

Cover: Book Cover Artistry by Heather Hamilton-Senter

PRAISE FOR
ERIN RICHARDS' BOOKS

"I loved this book [*Chasing Shadows*] and it never faltered from its action and suspense." ~*Night Owl Reviews* (NOR 5-Star Top Pick)

"The suspense will keep you turning the pages... The characters are complex and well-developed and there is never a dull moment in the story [*Chasing Shadows*]. If you love your romance with suspense, this is one book you need to read! 5 stars all the way!" ~*The Romance Reviews*

"*Stealing Twilight* by Erin Richards is completely enthralling with its addicting characters, unique plot, and satisfying ending." ~*Amazon 5-Star Review*

"*Seducing Darkness* is fast-paced and action-packed. It is well-written with vivid imagery that allowed me to get lost in the story. It offers drama, intrigue, and romance with a hint of humor that kept me entertained throughout." ~*Amazon 5-Star Review*

"Full of adventure, romance and two wonderfully heroic characters. The descriptions of the island are beautiful and the passion between Morgan and Ryan leaves you turning the pages to see if they can finally come together. A great book [*Wicked Paradise*]." ~*5-Stars, Paranormal Romance Guild*

"Perfect for fans of Julie Kagawa & Alyssa Rose Ivy. Loved this book [*Forbidden Thirteen*]! The plot was unique in a genre where everything has been done before. Just the perfect balance of action, supernatural and hot romance. Bring on book 2!" ~*5-Star Amazon Review*

BOOKS BY
ERIN RICHARDS

Psychic Justice Series
Chasing Shadows, Book 1
Twilight Rising, Book 2
Stealing Twilight, Book 3
Seducing Darkness, Book 4
Tempting Midnight, Book 5

Forbidden Legacy Series
Forbidden Thirteen, Book 1

Wilde Witches Series
Black Magic Rising, Book 1
Black Warlocks Prowling, Book 2
Black Curses Brewing, Book 3
Igniting the Witch, Prequel

Wicked Paradise

Young Adult
Vigilante Nights
Dragonfly Nightmare
Bittersweet Wreckage

See updated book list at:
www.erinrichards.com/booklist.htm

BLACK MAGIC
RISING

Chapter 1

The shadow oozed down her bare arm like thick, warm blood. Willow tapped Sage's shoulder twice, giving her oldest sister, the High Priestess of the Wilde West Coven, the pre-arranged signal. The thirteen witches closed the sacred circle, encapsulating Willow and the hulking shadow within the thirteen protective points. The prickly shadow stirred around her ankles, reaching ghostly fingers up her leg, goose bumps chasing the sinister caress. A briny breeze wafted around the circle. Sparks flickered up from the bonfire and dissipated in the night air like dying fireflies. *Why the hell can't this freaking shadow die as well?*

Sage's golden blonde hair floated in a halo around her head, and Willow focused on the undulating tresses. She ignored the chanting witches before she lost her concentration on the task at hand, which was letting the magic surrounding her aid in resisting the lure of evil and kill it off. The new moon hovered behind a thin veil of clouds. Another breeze trapped the specter on a flicker of candlelight from the lit candle in Willow's hand. The ghostly blob flitted away from the candlelight in obvious fear. Willow refused to take her gaze off the bastard.

The witches each lit a candle on the points of the circle, and the specter began a frenetic dance to escape the light, until it huddled flat and limp on the cool sand near Willow's feet in the center of the circle. Too close, too hungry. Willow took a half step away from it, stopping her movement after Sage shook her head. She grimaced and suffered the proximity to the piece of crap. *I'll get rid of the son of a black warlock if it's the last thing I do tonight.*

Waves rushed over the sand, then ebbed to escape a foamy oblivion on the shoreline. Willow barely heard the voices intoning the spell over the booming song of the Pacific. The flames on the candles madly danced in the sea air but remained strong. The shadow pressed closer, touching her legs and sending chills down her spine. Willow likened the shadow to a demon, not that she'd ever confronted a demon, not that they still existed. As far as she knew, no witch throughout time had ever succeeded in a warding spell on a demon—if that was what had latched on to Willow. Instead, they'd killed the demons outright hundreds of years ago. None of the coven witches had a clue. Would the spell even work? *It has to!* She was freaking tired of the douche-canoe chasing her all over California, between home in Santa Cruz and school in Santa Clara. It seeped into her senses, under her skin, broiled the very marrow of her bones, screwed with every facet of her life. Threatening, but not actually making good on the threat.

With the black candle in her hand, Willow lit the prepared pile of herbs, releasing the strong scent of rosemary. The shadow demon, whatever the hell thing, emitted a soft keening. An invisible force touched her neck in a lover's caress. Lust replaced the pain and evil that'd tormented her on and off for two months, and she fought the untimely and unnatural—forced—stirring of her desire.

Teeth clattering, she spoke her part of the spell, "Whatever evil comes to me here, I cast you back; I have no fear." Fire flared up from the smoldering herbs, and a briny sea breeze gusted through the circle of witches. Sage's blonde hair reached for Willow. Willow's long red hair escaped the confines of her band and fluttered in the wind behind her, as if trying to escape the reach of Sage's hair. "With the speed of wind and the dark of night, may all your harboring take flight." The shadow's keening evolved into a deafening roar, and Willow slapped her palms over her ears. "With the swiftness of the sea and all the power found in me, as I will, so mote it be." Sucking in a breath and raising her voice, she leaned forward, flicked her hand at the frantic shadow. "I cast you out. I cast you gone." With a gusty breath, she blew the candle flame at the cringing shadow. "Return to your origins!"

The witches shouted in unison, "Return to your origins, so mote it be."

Wind funnels erupted inside and around the circle, and the candles sputtered out. The pile of ashes and herbs blew into the faces of the witches. Arms waved and voices soared as the women staggered out of formation, wiping at their streaming eyes, fighting the gusts.

"Willow!" Sage yelled from what sounded like miles away.

Evil spread its taint over Willow, and a soft red glow emanated off her, turning into an inky blackness smothering her light, her life. The manifestation of evil engulfed her and rolled her onto her back onto the sand. Numb from scalp to toes, she fell into the land of nothing. Flashes of lightning burst in her skull. Crackles and pops drowned out the uproar of the witches and warlocks who feared to approach her. A tiny ball of fire hovered over her upraised right palm, wispy in a land between life and death.

A tendril of the shadow fondled Willow's cheek lovingly, seemed to press a kiss to her forehead, and whispered in a breezy voice, "Mine. Always. Forever."

The face of the handsome man who'd haunted her dreams for the last two months bloomed in her mind. Dark flowing hair, sparkling blue-green eyes, blade nose, and full sensuous lips. Evil and lust emanated off the specter, both stinging and sending her writhing to stop the desire suddenly throbbing through her lower regions. The shadow formed into the shape of the man, and he hovered over her, pressing closer, pinning her to the sand. It waited for her to do something. Confusion filled her mind.

"Who are you? Do you need my help?" she asked in her head. "Are you a ghost? I can't help spirits pass to the Shadowlands. That's not my thing." *Did she even have a thing?*

"I am no ghost. Come to me. I can awaken your magic." The breezy words pervaded her head. The weight eased off, but kept her anchored to the sand.

"Come on, Willow!" Someone shook her, and Sage's familiar commanding voice pulled her out of her trance.

The smothering evil lifted, and Willow's eyelids fluttered open. Concerned faces of the gaggle of witches and warlocks hovered above her. The ghostly evil floated away on a brackish sea breeze, taunting her as it drifted over the ocean, leaving her zapped on the sand. She flicked her hand to rid it of the weird, simmering fireball. The whole situation left her epically curious and only a little afraid.

Willow rubbed her blurred eyes, then braced her elbows in the sand, propping herself up. "Didn't work," she croaked out. "The little shit's gone, but not fucking forgotten. What the hell?" She held out her hands, and her sister tugged her up. Willow staggered forward into Sage's First Warlock and consort's arms. Rafael clenched her waist and held her upright before she planted her face in the sand again.

The warlock growled low in his throat. Willow quickly stepped away from him, loathing his touch, the touch of any warlock. Most times, their barely disguised lust and menace bewildered her, leaving her jittery. Their oxymoronic cold and warm reception of her had no basis. Except that she was an outcast witch. By choice, not by decree. They resented her because as the youngest Wilde witch, she refused to join the coven. Refused to accept a warlock or even take one to her bed. Warlocks received power and status from a witch, and there were too few witches for the horde of available warlocks. Too few witches in the Wilde West Coven, aka, Wilde Coven, the most powerful and sought-after coven in the West. Willow was an über hot commodity. *Yay, me, Glenda the good witch. Not.*

Wasting her breath, she'd earlier told Sage she didn't want too many warlocks at the ceremony, but Sage couldn't go anywhere without an entourage of hulking hunks. And Sage certainly wouldn't risk thirteen witches together without the protection of an army of warlock guards, especially among a coven of mostly sisters, cousins, and aunts. Not that the Wilde Coven didn't include non-relatives, but they were far and few between with their huge family of female witches. The coven's inner circle vetted outsiders to the nth degree. By the time the coven allowed in a new witch, the witch was considered family.

The Witches Council laws required a heavy contingent of guards on any coven of thirteen witches and a High Priestess. Another oxymoron move on their chessboard since warlocks derived their power from the witch who bonded him. Warlocks possessed no power of their own. A not-so-insignificant issue that still created a shitstorm of bitterness and disdain at times amongst both witches and warlocks. Another reason Willow steered clear of anything related to witchery. She didn't need the drama. However, once a witch bonded a warlock, her powers became his and transformed the warlock into a magical killing machine. Once the witch died, a warlock lost his powers until bonded by another witch. A damn strong incentive to guard their witches well. Only a strong High Priestess could bond up to thirteen warlocks, or was even allowed to bond more than three warlocks. Sage's personal heaven.

They all creeped Willow out. *Why am I even thinking about this? It's not like I'll be joining the coven anytime soon. I like my island of one.* Willow shook off her thoughts and jerked her chin out of Sage's grip.

"What happened? Have you ever blacked out?" Sage's sultry tone grew shrill. "Did you invoke magic?" She guided Willow away from the others, following a beam of light streaming from Rafael's finger, wielding Sage's witch-fire, the most powerful element derived from her aether, the mother of all powers. The only magical element she allowed her warlocks to use, which led Willow to believe Sage wasn't so great with her other elements stemming from aether.

Willow snagged her leather motorcycle jacket off a beach chair and shrugged it on. "Like you've ever done a banishing ritual on a shadow demon or any demon for that matter? If it is a demon. What is the blasted thing, anyways? Why's it tailgating me?" Willow straightened her twisted T-shirt beneath her jacket. "And do I have to *spell* it out again? Witchcraft and I don't live on the same island. Haven't I tanked enough spells?" The weird fireball on her hand arose in her memory. Did that magic belong to the *thing*? Far as she knew, her magic, whenever it deigned to make a half-assed appearance, was witch-water. She'd dampened enough things to find her supposed innate water element annoying as hell. Even though she didn't want the drama of the coven, she wanted full access to her stupid magic. Every other witch she knew had wielded some magic by the time the witch was thirteen, and all had gained full-blown powers by their eighteenth birthday. Willow felt her magic sloshing around inside her and knew she had it. But it hid deep in her core, as if waiting for something, or someone, to summon it out of hiding for good.

Sage swatted Willow's arm. "What'd you see when you conked out?" She flicked a blade of seagrass out of Willow's hair.

Willow shrugged. The slash of light lent Sage's face a ghostly outline. "I didn't *conk* out. Whackjob shadow dumped me in a trance." The moment the words left her mouth, she knew how batshit crazy she sounded. But the idea didn't halt the ice-cold apprehension deluging her bones, nearly buckling her knees. Rafael snaked out an arm to catch her if she fell. Shuddering, Willow sidestepped his constant hovering.

She told Sage what she'd heard, how she'd felt. "This isn't witchcraft. Something attacked me, the same being tailing me for two months." She focused on the pointy ear of Sage's white owl familiar sticking out of the top of her blouse, and shivered again, unsure whether her cold stemmed from the January night on the Santa Cruz beach or the evil she couldn't shake. Or the confusing illuminations gleaned that night.

"I don't want you alone until we banish this bitch." Sage held up her hand to stop Rafael from stalking them too close, cognizant of Willow's wariness of her warlocks. "Stay with us on the beach. Then you can go to the covenstead with me."

The bonfire's amber waves rolled toward the misty sky as if chasing the departing shadow. Willow studied the other witches and their warlocks getting down to serious drinking and partying. Two of Sage's bonded warlocks were kissing, arms and legs tangled, rolling on the sand. Willow's palms dampened, and she fought the compulsion to ogle the orgies the Wilde witches never tired of.

"Hell to the no." Crimson, her butterfly familiar, frantically moved from one breast to the other, whipping her hormones into a tizzy. Arms across her chest to ward off the cold, Willow walked off, trying to press Crimson back into tattoo form to still its movements. *Chill, Crimson. I don't need you stirring my senses right now.*

A witch's familiar was like a witch's right hand to aid a witch in using and wielding magic. A familiar also helped diagnose illnesses, identified and created emotions, and aided in bewitchment and protection of a witch. They were used for divining and finding lost objects and treasures, conjured in rituals and spells, and least not, used in bonding warlocks to a witch. Every witch who turned sixteen gained smaller, less magical bonding familiars just for the purpose of snagging a warlock into the witch's personal realm. Willow's bonding familiar, Rosebud, twittered against her skin as if it was preparing to emerge for the first time. Preparing to begin a new life with a bonded warlock. As if that warlock was near. *What the freakass hell?* Willow smacked down on the small butterfly tattoo, trying to halt the weird sensations.

Sage's footsteps slogged in the sand behind her. "Willow! You don't have to partake in the festivities. Stay safe here. We'll figure it out. I need to know what's going on, if there're any threats to the coven." Sage sighed heavily. "If you'd pledge your fealty, things would be different. We've never had a witch in the family voluntarily cast herself out. We can't help you if you keep running." Sage laughed bitterly. "You're ruining our rep."

Her sister's words fell on deaf ears. She'd thwarted the

Witches Council and the Wilde West Coven's rules *and* the odds, and didn't give a rat's ass that she was different. *Join the coven, pledge fealty, bond a warlock. Dominate him. Blah, blah, blah. Rinse and repeat.*

"I'll take her home and guard her," a deep sensuous voice wafted out of the fog forming on the beach, blurring the stars twinkling overhead. His all-too-familiar voice drove a skittering tingle up Willow's spine and sent Crimson into a frenetic dance across her breasts. Rosebud quivered on her skin. Heat flared up her neck and bathed her face. A renewed embarrassment dropped anchor in her gut. She should've expected Evan Ravenwood to attend and guard Sage tonight. Why hadn't she noticed him earlier?

Rafael appeared behind Sage and pressed himself to her like a leech. He growled his stupidass dominant growl, making some dumb unspoken point from his repertoire of Neanderthal opinions Willow never understood.

Evan stood three feet behind Rafael, the ever-obedient, lower-caste warlock. The large dark silhouette hid the gorgeous hunk Sage had dug up somewhere before Summer Solstice and added him to her warlock entourage. Totally her type. *Why break the mold?*

The idea of Sage's cavemen warlocks bending their will to a witch sent Willow twitching like a witch with a full-body rash. *So unnatural, so assbackwards. So why she didn't belong.*

"Evan." Sage flicked her hand, and a white owl flew off her fingers, summoning him forward. Once a familiar left its tattoo form on a witch's body, it became real until it reformed onto skin. Her summoning familiar formed on Evan's bare chest as a white tattoo, startling against his deep tan. He strutted forward into the light Rafael produced from his witch-fire. The owl returned to Sage and sank onto the back of her hand.

Of course he's bare-chested. Sage's demands and rules

for her coven were as consistent as the Milky Way. The less clothes, the better. Willow took Evan in from his bare feet up his skintight jeans, devouring his romance-novel, six-pack abs and wide-muscled chest. Disgust roiled in her stomach at the cliché he represented, the indignities he'd suffered at Sage's whims, his dominant master, er, mistress. The obedient dog. The way of the Wilde Coven. The way of all 21st-century witches and warlocks. If Willow could change that mold, she might belong to their world. Until then, an outcast she'd remain, no matter that Evan confused her more than any man or warlock she'd ever met, especially after their stupid drunken and blind kiss at Summer Solstice. *Did Evan even know he'd kissed me? Did he know how easily I had responded to that kiss?*

Chapter 2

Evan swallowed down a fiery lump of awkwardness and a slew of other emotions. Too many days had elapsed since Sage had accepted him into the Wilde Coven. He dreaded the unfolding scene even as he'd counted down the days to its inevitability. Counted down the days he'd lay his gaze upon Willow Wilde once again, the witch who'd haunted him since the Wilde inner circle had initiated him and three other warlocks into the coven, during the Summer Solstice event. The day he'd accepted his second master.

The lesser of two evils.

Disconcertingly and tickling his flesh, Jet, his bald eagle familiar, lifted off his leg and flapped his wings against Evan's thigh where he'd banished the familiar before removing his shirt, per Sage's dumb rules. Removing his shirt revealed too much to her perpetually lusting eyes. The bald eagle revealed even more. Enough to get him killed.

Did Willow recognize me? Did she know I was the one she'd called Nathan? Summer Solstice... she'd pressed both hands to his pectorals that fateful night, stirring something deep inside him. Jet had gone wild, and Evan had nearly lost it trying to keep his familiar from stirring more than the hairs on his thigh. Between Jet and his damn lust, he'd almost lost his shit when Willow had pressed her lips to his and her tongue nudged his mouth apart. The sweet taste of whiskey on her breath mated with the bourbon on his tongue, a fiery concoction he thought would light up the inky darkness of the covenstead's yard and reveal his identity. All he'd wanted was to melt her ice to discover the fire in her core.

Even though their kiss had ignited an insatiable fire within him, he'd pulled away from her. If either of his masters had discovered he'd kissed Willow Wilde, death might have been too easy of a penalty. But Willow had crawled onto his lap and brushed her luscious breasts against his bare chest. Whimpering, she refused to let him push her away, and her lips met his parted and willing mouth again. He let her drown herself in him. Not that it was a sacrifice, quite the contrary. He had Willow Wilde exactly where he wanted her. It was just too soon, way too soon to exact his plan. The vanilla, slightly flowery scent of her had stirred his lust almost to the point of no return.

But that long-in-the-making plan had whacked him upside the head. He'd gripped her hips and gently set her off his lap onto the verdant lawn. He hadn't expected her to kiss him. Alcohol had killed her guard and inhibitions. He'd drunk enough alcohol to prevent him from walking away and accepting what she offered at first. A kiss. One simple kiss. "Come on, Nathan. Just one night," she'd said with a pout to her voice. "I know you want me. Just no strings, okay? I can't do strings. But I need you right now. I need *sexxx*," she slurred her words.

Reality had done another brutal number to the side of Evan's head. He'd stood abruptly and turned away from the sight of her willowy form stretching out on the grass, her auburn hair a mantle of ink framing her face. Hair he wanted to sift his fingers through. "Not like this, Willow. I can't—" He'd fled the scene that had haunted him for over six months.

He had no idea if she'd ever figured it out. Took him only a day to learn Nathan was a warlock who'd left the coven not long after Evan had joined.

And there was nothing simple about that kiss.

Standing on the beach, gazing upon Willow for the first time since that summer night, his mouth had run amuck, and he'd volunteered to guard her when his head should have forced his legs to beat a hasty retreat far from the nightmare about to unfurl.

Jet's razor-sharp beak bit Evan's thigh, and he choked down a painful wince. *Son of a bald eagle, Jet. Knock it off.* The moment he tossed the mental command to his familiar, the unmistakable tingle of black magic joined the damp coastal air. His familiar had been warning him when his head was stuck up his ass over his predicament. Too late. He'd let up on his guard too late to shield Sage and Willow from the attack. The black magic didn't stem from him, but his magic joined the attack as if he'd instigated it, leaving his feet wedged in heavy sand up to his ankles, trapping him in place like it was cement. Black magic drew from its own kind, and there was no stopping the mingling with his innate magic. At least he hadn't yet figured out how to avoid the pull. *Yet.*

Swift and furious, a downpour of electricity flickered like falling stars over Sage, Willow, and Rafael. Rafael tried to thwart the electricity by fighting it with fire, but sand blew up from Evan's feet and blew Rafael's witch-fire asunder. The other warlock scrambled to stop the sand from blowing, the stars from exploding, but the strong black magic had usurped his own magic, leaving him depleted and panting. Using his body, his only defense against the firestorm, Rafael tried to block the onslaught from touching Sage and Willow. The stars exploded into flaming blasts in the air above them, and embers rained down onto them, singeing skin and clothes.

Sage screamed a string of curses and tried to invoke her fire magic in a defensive attack, but despite her more powerful aether-infused witch-fire, fire met fire and the black magic burned through the streams of lightning shooting in swirls off her fingers. Rafael pushed her to the ground and smothered her with his body to protect her.

"Down now, Willow," Rafael bellowed, trying to pull her down. But she evaded him and escaped his reach.

Mesmerized, Willow stood, her feet rooted to the sand, arms outstretched as if to welcome the stars home. The sparks quit raining upon her and hovered over her head, swirling in a tempest as if her hidden magic had finally emerged into a freaky hidden ability.

"Get her, Rafael. Evan, do something!" Blowing sand muffled Sage's chasing scream.

Stars and sand twisted and sparked, and then mushroomed above Willow's head like a nuclear cloud. Evan tried to pull his magic back, but he'd lost control. The foreign black magic prevailed, locked on to him, tugging unrestrained magic out of him. He finally pulled his feet out of the sand and gathered Willow in his arms. The moment he touched her, cinders fell from the sky again and sprayed his back, torched tiny holes in Willow's leather jacket.

"Don't touch me!" Willow pushed at him. "It will go away. Just back off, idiot warlock."

He took no offense at Willow's not-so-endearment, because he *was* an *idiot* to allow thoughts of Willow to kill his purpose, his one lousy job. He may as well kiss his ass goodbye now, since one master or the other would kick him to the curb, especially if Willow got hurt—or worse—on his watch. Evan dropped his arms, but refused to back away from her. He needed close proximity in case the threat worsened.

Rafael and Sage remained on the ground, their magic useless, or else they feared their interference too treacherous.

Waves booming on the shore became the only sound on the beach as the revelry of the witches and warlocks had crashed into a pinprick of nothing. They all watched and waited from a distance, unable to lift a finger to stop the foreign magic attack. Several witches, in all states of dress, or no dress, gathered together, lighting candles, preparing a banishing spell, and forming a circle. One black-haired witch leafed like mad through a spell book as a warlock held his phone flashlight over her shoulder, a beacon of sanity. Evan knew it was a waste of time. Only a few spell books in existence documented black spells. Only a black spell could kill another black spell. Only one of Evan's masters possessed a Book of Ink and Shadows. That master was not Sage Wilde.

Evan took in the peripheral scene quickly, before his gaze bounced back to Willow and the cloud of sand and stars revolving above her head. She stood immovable, as if waiting for the right moment to say, "Beam me up, Scotty." The cool breeze swept over the fear burning down his back.

Eyes closed and head tilted back, Willow's arms remained outstretched. She appeared to tame the treacherous cloud. The increasing burnt-metal tang of black magic reigned. It sneered at Willow's paltry attempt to thwart it, let alone master it. The black magic expanded and thrust a barrier of fire around Willow. The pull of power from Evan nearly knocked him down, and he staggered drunkenly against the invisible barrier to regain his composure. Sage cast angry eyes upon him, her anger joining her pale fear. Anytime he used her fire magic, she knew, and she felt it now. *What the hell am I going to do?*

"Kill the magic, Evan. You're making it worse!" Sage's voice infiltrated his head.

Did she think he was trying to fight the attack? *Well, hell. Let her think it. Her erroneous thoughts may save my ass.*

"I'm stopping the magic from touching her. It's strong." True that.

Evan exerted all his effort to redirect the fire around Willow, or made it look like he was keeping it from touching her, all the while fighting the black magic with every fiber of his being. The dirty magic pulled on his witch-fire and he yanked the thread back. It yanked harder, and he groaned from the effort of letting a little of it slip away while making it appear to Sage that he battled the threat, using her bonded magic. The effort of obeying two masters was killing him. If this night didn't hammer his stupid mess into his head, nothing would. The time had come to mix it up and take control. His way.

Willow's arms fluttered lifelessly down to her sides before she bolstered them again, outstretched above her head, palms facing the sky. The cloud of sparking stars and dense sand continued swirling above her. Lines strained her forehead, and the heat from the cyclone of fire turned her face scarlet.

Evan wanted nothing more than to take her in his arms and whisk her away from the two worlds that desperately coveted her. He wanted to show her another choice, a better choice. His world. Or a new world of their own making.

The fire barrier encapsulating Willow thickened. Despite the sea breeze, sweat trickled down his bare chest, soaking the waistband of his jeans. The agony of defeat thundered through his head. Water wet his hair, traveled down his back. He didn't realize the drizzle had turned to rain until he shook his head to fling the moisture out of his eyes.

The ring of fire sizzled and began to sputter out, granting him the chance he needed. He leaped through the dying fire toward Willow. He scooped her into his arms and dove through the other side of the dwindling fire ring. She wrapped her arms around his neck, her head lolling on his shoulder. Heaving in air, Evan stumbled to the sand and fell on his knees, Willow nestled in his arms. The welcome rain cooled their overheated bodies.

The cloud of stars and sand rained down upon the black spot of sand where it had held Willow hostage. A puff of smoke mushroomed up from the ground and splintered into wisps high above their heads.

The rain ceased abruptly. Willow lifted her head, and her gaze latched on to his face. Fear ravaged her eyes, and she began to shake in his arms. Evan tightened his clinch around her, his heart galloping as if it would explode out of his rib cage. Jet cooed contentedly from his thigh.

"Willow, hon, are you okay?" Sage's voice broke through the sound of his thundering heart and the hitching of Willow's breath.

Sage and Rafael knelt before Evan and Willow, Sage's hands cupping Willow's face. Not a drop of rain had marred Willow's beautiful perfection.

Chapter 3

Willow's gaze inched up from Evan's broad chest to his chiseled face, the scariest warlock she'd ever seen. And hottest. No wonder Sage had bonded him as part of her gang of minions-slash-guards. He'd scare the bejeezus out of anyone threatening to hurt a coven member. In the light Rafael wielded, she made out his features. Mesmerizing, lethal, so freaking gorgeous in a rugged and frosty godlike way. Dark, wet hair framed his tanned face, and piercing gray-blue eyes started to smolder like black ice, probing every inch of her face. Strands of his shoulder-length hair were hooked on his right eyelash, and she wanted to sweep them away. Willow licked her lips, holding in the fire he'd ignited in her southern region. *Or am I suffering from the scorching effects of the fire magic? Whatever. Neither fire nor Evan need apply for access to her body. No free passes granted.*

Willow pushed against Evan's bare chest and steely arms. "I'm fine. Let me go."

Crimson fluttered off Willow without permission and nestled between Evan's shoulder and neck for the barest moment, like a kiss, before Willow's skin reabsorbed her familiar. *Hello? What the heck?* Familiars didn't normally take off and do their own thing, unless it was to protect its witch. In this case, if Evan was evil or intent on harming her, Crimson would have bitten him, injecting its poison to subdue him. *Not freaking kiss him! Holy hell in a handbasket.*

Rafael towered over her. He held out his arm and she gripped it, leveraging off the sand and off Evan's too enticing lap.

Evan jumped up, ready to catch her, while she gained her balance. Not that her wobbly legs gave any semblance of a steady balance. Maybe Evan might catch her if she fell. One could only wish. *Whoa. What? Where did that wish stem from?* Willow slapped her palm against the side of her head, trying to slap her brain cells back to life. Arm still weak from holding it aloft, she clutched her aching and thoroughly baffled head. When her fingers slid into her damp hair, she began to tremble. What had she done? Better yet, what had Evan done to her? She had followed the source of magic to Evan, or at least some of it. And it wasn't him wielding Sage's magic like a good little warlock had the capability to do. Where had the second source of magic stemmed from? Confusion further muddled her mind.

"Willow, are you okay?" His brusque voice raked down her back, his fingers chasing the voice, a bare breeze of a touch that sent a quiver down her spine.

"Back off." Fear lanced her, and she stepped away from him, bumped into Rafael. He handed her a beach towel and she wrapped it around herself, pulling the edges tight as if to ward off his warlock cooties.

"Come to me, Evan," Sage ordered, and her summoning owl flew to him. Growling, Rafael edged closer to Sage.

Ducking her head, Willow hid a smile. Rafael hated that Sage refused to commit to him, leaving her doors wide open to all her minions, warlock or witch.

The small white owl tattoo tore off Evan's skin and returned to cover the back of Sage's right hand. Evan wrapped an arm around Sage's waist, forcing Rafael to stand down. His witch light changed to a sword of fire to accompany his growl of dislike. Even though Rafael was Sage's number one warlock and top consort, as High Priestess, she had the right to screw anything in sight, including all her bonded warlocks. Rafael had no choice but to accept it, or leave his post as the most powerful warlock in the West. It was the way of the coven. Willow almost felt sorry for him. Almost.

Sage gripped Evan's chin. Her lips landed on his and she kissed him, tongue digging for his Adam's apple. "Thank you for saving my sister."

Leave it to Sage to flip a troublesome situation around to sex. Unable to witness her nymphomaniac sister's disgusting display of ridiculous power and dominance, Willow stared out toward the black ocean, tried to center her mind. As her gaze shifted, she caught Rafael's pained grimace. He loved Sage so much and wanted her exclusively, even though he knew what it meant to be Sage Wilde's warlock. He was First Warlock, but not the only warlock. He ruled her warlocks as her second-in-command. Although he always butted heads with Willow, she knew he was good for Sage, for the whole coven. Time their High Priestess grew the hell up and opened her eyes to what he offered.

A low murmur and rustling arose to Willow's right as the coven's witches and warlocks packed up. Willow and her predicament with a capital "P" had thoroughly crashed their night of merriment.

"Willow." A wand of sparkles touched Willow's arm

before Sage withdrew her witch-fire. "Answer me. Are you okay?" Willow searched for words, not so much to describe what had just happened to her, but the words to distract her sister until she understood the insanity herself. "Look at me," Sage commanded in the powerful tone as the leader of the Western Witch's Council, not merely the leader of the Wilde West Coven.

Slowly, she faced Sage, who was now draped all over Evan, a cougar enthralling the unwary young. Her sister's billowy black blouse had slipped off her shoulder, exposing her right breast to the top of her nipple. Breasts that had spurred an entire army of warlocks to grovel at her feet for their taste of Sage, her magic, her power. Most warlocks would give their right nut to replace Rafael. Willow forced her gaze from slipping to Evan, from his raw magnetism that both scared the crap out of her and flipped the switch on *her* budding nymphomania. After all, she had an excellent role model in Sage.

"You don't command me, remember?" Willow finally said. "I'm not one of your minions or playthings." She shot a glance at Evan's stoic, frozen mien, and hid her surprise when the slightest smile tugged up the corners of his lips.

"I'm the head of the family and I want you safe. I promised"—her voice hitched—"Mom and Dad that I'd always protect you, no matter if you joined the coven or not. Do you see why you need me... us?" Sage wanded her outstretched arm to encompass the silent group of witches and warlocks surrounding them, waiting and watching. Evan released Sage, and she moved into Willow's bubble of space, pulling her blouse up to her shoulder. Willow backed up a step. Sage pressed forward. "Evan will take you home and remain with you until I figure this out. I'll skim through the Book of Shadows and tomes on black magic tonight."

"What if Evan doesn't want to play babysitter?" Willow

taunted her sister, hating that Sage had resorted to baiting her with their dead parents, and knowing Evan would do her bidding until the day Sage broke their bond, or death, whichever came first. *Oh, and he'd already volunteered. Check that.*

"Oh, but I do." His smooth baritone brought a blush to Willow's already inflamed cheeks. His sincerity shook her, disconcerting, almost possessive. She could hardly contain Crimson's fluttering excitement on her breasts. Gritting her teeth, she slapped her hand over her heart, smacking her familiar into submission.

Sage smiled. "There. It's all settled." She leaned down from her towering five-nine height to whisper in Willow's ear. "Have fun with him tonight. You need a good lay. All college work all the time makes for a dull witch. No wonder you haven't awakened your magic. You don't allow yourself the pleasures of life to open yourself up to the elements." Her deep-throated laugh swelled in Willow's face.

Willow shoved Sage away, and both cavemen rushed to their master, muscles bulging and magic shimmering in the air. Sage held up a hand, signifying she was okay.

"No, thanks. I don't want your leftovers." Willow clenched her teeth.

"I didn't bond him for his magnificent package." Her eyes strayed to Evan's crotch and back to Willow. "I bonded him for his strength and ability. Next to Rafael, he wields my witch-fire better than any warlock I've ever bonded. That fire saved you tonight." She sobered. "Go. He'll keep you safe if you don't want to use your own magic."

"You know my magic sucks," Willow gritted out, hating the insinuations Sage loaded on her. If Sage hadn't figured it out, then maybe Willow had imagined the sensation of water meeting fire and dancing a strange tango inside her core. Her water? Evan's fire? Or what? She needed to figure it out. Away from Sage, away from the coven. Away from

Evan... or not. "Fine. What-the-fuck-ever."

Grabbing her sneakers, Willow slogged through the cold sand toward the hill. By the time she took her first step up the stairs leading to the parking lot, Evan tailgated her, pulling on his T-shirt. She ran up the million steps and stopped at her late-model Lexus.

"Want me to drive, mistress?"

"No! And I'm not your damn mistress!" *Goddess alive, save me from this torture.* "No one drives my car, except me."

"Nice car for a college kid."

A seething fury took hold of her intestines, curling and roiling inside her gut. "I'm twenty-four, Evan. Third-year law, graduating in the spring. What're you? Forty?" He didn't look a day older than her, too young for thirty-year-old Sage.

"Twenty-six," he grunted out. "Kidding, trying to lighten the mood. Didn't know you had a complex."

Fists curled, she spun on him, blinked rapidly, not believing the gorgeous smile transforming his face into swoon-worthy territory. Her mouth gaped, and a flush swept up her chest. A cold shower was on tap later. Or a dip into the Pacific Ocean. The warlock exuded such charisma, she wasn't sure if he'd glamoured her. Had her sister asked him to spell her to calm her down and accept his guard? Not that being near badass warlocks calmed her down. Usually the opposite. She pretty much steered clear of them. Didn't need them, didn't want the hassle, and certainly didn't want one bonded to her and calling her *mistress.* Too old-fashioned. For goddess' sake, welcome to the 21st century!

But this badass warlock might be her ticket to helping her unearth her magic. Not that she planned to fess up her ulterior motives to him.

"Just get in and zip it." She crawled into her car and

started the engine.

The car was inching toward the street before Evan shut his door. He remained silent, his lethal body absorbing the interior cab space. Oddly, his presence did comfort her, and peace threaded through her insides as her mind orbited her quandry. At least he'd zipped it. Warlocks were taught to defer to a witch in all ways, no matter if bonded to her or not. *It is what it is.* At the moment, coven law suited her. *Hypocrite much?*

The night had betrayed her royally. She'd expected her sister to vanquish the spell, allowing Willow to ride off into the moonglow, alone and free of evil. Willow would've paid the fee Sage exacted in legal work once she earned her law degree and passed the bar exam. Until then, Sage would use every advantage to coerce Willow to join the coven she'd shunned since she was eighteen. Willow had expected it. Now what?

The annoyance and sometimes pain of the black magic spell had driven Willow to seek the coven's help. She'd taken a huge leap approaching Sage, knowing there would be consequences and *quid pro quo*. What little witchcraft she'd tried as the stupidest witch in the West, had gone wonky to the point she hadn't practiced any craft in the two months the black spell had invaded her. She'd tried everything in her tiny arsenal to vanquish the spell, to no avail. At times, the *being* was erotic, most times black smut made her feel dirty and plain exhausted from the power it sucked off her. Yet, the magic threatening her on the beach hadn't sucked any power off her. Where had that power stemmed from? From the other witches? Not one witch said a word about a leech in power. Willow shivered, not from her damp clothes, but from the implications of the source of the various magics displayed that night. Until her sister figured out how to vanquish the *thing* seeping into her mind and body, nearly possessing her, she was saddled with Evan. Saddled with the shadow's words, *"I can awaken your magic."*

She white-knuckled the steering wheel, drove over the center line, and swerved to the right to avoid a head-on with a puny hybrid.

Evan's head bonked the window, and he grunted.

"Sorry," she grumbled, breathed in deeply and counted to ten. "I'm sorry I'm being such a bitch. Has nothing to do with you."

"Just the fact that a warlock is sitting in your car?"

His silky voice feathered across her skin. *Son of a witch.* "A little," she gritted out, fighting the new arousal attacking her. *What in the Hades is wrong with me?* Maybe Sage was right and she needed to get down and dirty for a change.

Law school and her part-time legal internship kept her busy, leaving no time to think about her lack of magic. And she certainly didn't need a man in her business. Bad enough lawyers and other interns constantly hit on her, but she didn't want to mix her personal life with her work and school life. Which meant her love life was pretty much in the toilet. By her choice. Did she really want more?

Shit, she wailed in her head. The night had flipped into a total epic fail, and now her hormones were sending out invitations to... Evan. She slapped the steering wheel.

"Something wrong?" the source of her consternation asked.

Yes. Peel off your pants and screw this bastard out of me and some sense into me. "I'm fine." She inhaled his spicy scent spiraling through her nostrils. Willow parked her car in her designated slot in her apartment complex garage. Did Sage have mind-reading abilities she passed on to her warlocks? *Just kill me now if she did.*

In that moment, she blissfully realized the black spell had remained at the beach since Evan had entered her bubble of personal space. Was this the reason Sage sent him to protect her? Was he imbued with banishing ability? Or was it something even more intriguing? Feathers danced up her backside where his fingers had danced earlier.

"Why don't you live closer to campus?" He jerked her out of her crazed thoughts.

"Too many people in the Bay Area."

"Then why not live on the Wilde covenstead?"

"Too many people there too. It's winter break. I commute. It works."

Her parents had left her enough trust money for college, a car, an apartment, and a living stipend for a good long time. The trust fund gave Willow her dearly prized independence. Sage hated it.

Before she'd even unbuckled her seat belt, Evan had jogged around the car and opened her door. The hard evidence of his arousal hit her sight, front and center. She licked her lips, fighting the horror of her attraction to her sister's lover, the attraction to a stranger, most of all the lure to a warlock and all the repercussions he represented. Repercussions she'd fought since her age of majority at eighteen. The time she should've gained her full power as a witch. The biggest epic failure in her game of life. At least she had a promising law career.

Reluctantly, she took Evan's proffered hand, and he gloved her hand in his warmth. He pulled her out, and she stumbled against his body, not shielding her from the biggest, hardest erection she'd ever felt pressed against her middle. It was like he was offering a sampling of the merchandise to the highest bidder. Normally, feeling up a warlock grossed her out, but the night had already catapulted her into the twilight zone. On top of that, his intangible charisma engulfed her, shooting an unfamiliar thrill through her lower torso.

Instead of backing off, she molded herself closer to him. His spicy cologne mixed with his natural scent created a stirring in her senses. Fingers lingered over his damp jeans before she trailed them up his chest. What harm was there in touching? Sage said play with him. Didn't mean she had to screw his brains out. She didn't take seconds from her sister. But the idea of Evan's obvious lust and his large hands affixed on her hips set off such an unfamiliar craving.

Most of all, she had the wildest urge to make him denounce his bond to Sage and become Willow's equal. Could she turn the tide for all witches and warlocks? Could she find the magic to create equality between them instead of this dance of dominance witches held over their warlocks' heads?

Parking lot lights burned down the darkness, putting them on display in the otherwise dark lot. Nearing midnight, some apartment windows had gone dark, others blazed with Friday night college life.

"Chill, Willow," Evan said, his words pebbly. "Let's take it inside where it's safe."

Willow's fingers froze and her horror jammed her spine against the car. What the heck was she thinking? He belonged to Sage, for Pete's sake! A shudder rolled up from her toes. Something about him left her dying to abandon all she believed in for one night of hot and wild sex. *Holy confused head!*

She had no ability to bond another witch's warlock. She had no magic to offer him even if she wanted to bond him, let alone become his equal. Willow jerked her hand away as if singed, shoved past him, and dashed toward the lobby doors. The car door slammed, and Evan's footsteps pounded behind her.

The deadbolt on her apartment door stuck, and Evan's strong hand gloved hers again, flickering lightning up her arm. Seriously, real flickers of lightning, shooting from where their skin made contact, and lighting the dim hallway outside her door. Streaks lit her up from the inside out, layering black smut in her chest. A different black smut than before, lighter and non-evasive. It evaporated the strange sensation of water sloshing around inside her, dousing what little magic she possessed.

Chapter 4

Blinking up a breeze, Willow froze. Evan wasn't wielding Sage's magic. Sage's warlocks who brandished her fire magic didn't create electric friction with other witches. Nor was this alien magic derived from Willow's paltry unknown magic—whatever magic she possessed. Earlier, she thought she'd used witch-fire for a moment, which was ludicrous. She'd always known her elemental magic was water. If she had full control of her magic, witch-water would douse any witch-fire directed at her, let alone in her. Not that she held any illusions that she possessed two elements. Nope. Not her, the lamest witch in the West. *What new alternate universe did I stumble into?*

"Um, dude, what was that?" Shaking her hands as if to shake off magic dripping from her fingers, she plastered herself to the door to distance herself from the hulking warlock on her tail.

Evan coughed into his shoulder, trying to smother his liars-who-lie words. "Sage's magic."

"Try again." Willow prodded the door open and sprang

through the opening, preparing to slam the door on his lying face. The loathsome black spell flared to life again, dizzying her, its malevolence attacking her already swirling gut. The smutty magic definitely stemmed from Evan. This time she knew for sure. Something was off about him. Not evil, not good either. Not Sage's magic. Willow knew what Sage's magic felt like, as well as the faint telltale scent of burning sage, her namesake. *Evan? A warlock who wielded his own magic? No freaking way.*

Another round of horror stalled her heartbeat, and she slammed the door on his large booted foot wedged between the door and jamb. "Whoa. Wait. *You* planted the black spell on me? So you banished the spell earlier and just re-invoked it? Who are you? *What* are you? What the freaking hell do you want from me?" Was Sage faking her out and using Evan to get Willow into the coven? *What the ever-loving hell? Would Sage stoop to that level?*

Willow attempted to raise her useless water magic to wash him away from the door. A mist rose inside her, leaving one lone rivulet to drip off her right pointer finger with an odd spark chaser. She shook her hand, shaking a few more tiny drops of water and embers away. Was she channeling a bit of his witch-fire, ala Sage's witch-fire? *Crap-ass magic!*

"It's not what you think," he said too cool. Too deadly.

"Tell me what I think, then." The electric pulses he generated with the black spell in full attack mode dried up her witch-water. Not that she needed the black spell to kill her own magic. She'd mastered that all on her own. The black smut sparked tiny fires inside her blood, her bones, moving from her head to her toes and everywhere in between. Every drop of moisture in her body seemed to wither into a dust bowl, leaving her wanting to dunk herself into a cauldron of melting ice cubes.

"I'm stronger than most warlocks. Sage told you." Evan

paused and captured her gaze as if gauging her reaction. "And I derive power of my own." The low-spoken words hung heavy in the air. He slid his gaze to his feet, across the room, anywhere but on her. "The Wilde Coven's suffering from attacks by other covens in a power play for the West. They need stronger warlocks to prevail. It's part why I agreed to join the coven. I can help."

"Give me a break." Willow shook her head, a sneer traversing her face. "Warlocks derive no magic other than what their bonded witch spoon-feeds them." Only a black warlock possessed innate magic. She waved a dismissive hand, but she remembered Sage yakking about other witches in both her coven and other covens suffering from black magic attacks. A trio of witches had managed to vanquish the other spells on Sage's witches, unlike Willow's spell, which a full circle of thirteen witches couldn't touch.

What Evan insinuated landed on the flip side of sanity. Witches had abolished the last black warlocks over a hundred years ago. And Sage never mentioned anything about threats to the Wilde Coven from other covens.

Black warlocks. No way. They're extinct. She scratched her head. *Marbles come home to roost!*

From what she'd memorized from her warlock history during her early teen witch's training, a black warlock had the ability to totally bind a witch's magic and bespell any witch as well as use the witch's power against her. Unlike a witch bonding a warlock and retaining an ability to release him from her bond, a black warlock's spells booted the witch under his dominance as a marked minion for life. A black warlock could stop a witch from using magic. He could make a witch do nearly anything at his discretion, all the while strengthening his magic with hers.

Bile rose and her gaze locked on the trash can by her desk. She darted toward the can. Didn't matter that she'd released the door. If a black warlock had spelled her, he'd find her anywhere, on Earth or in the Milky Way, stopped by no measly door. Evan stomped inside her studio apartment and banged the door shut, towering over her petite five-five frame bent over her trash can full of crumpled balls of paper. So much for her legal brief assignment. She dry-heaved from her already empty stomach. The legal brief lucked out and remained intact.

After a few seconds to wrap her mind around her insanity of the moment, Willow swallowed hard and straightened to her full height. "Tell me what's going on or I swear I'll blow a hole through you," she managed to croak out through a hoarse throat. Not sure how she'd accomplish her threat with her gun hidden in the bathroom, but the warning sounded A-okay in her new witch-verse.

"Let me explain." Evan extended a hand, his arm muscles bulging. Willow feasted on the arm strong enough to snap her in two. It entranced her, terrorized her. Most of all, she wanted to run her fingers over the solid ropes of his bronzed muscles. Wanted his arm holding her to his hard body.

Gah, she railed inside her tangled mind. "What kind of spell did you dump on me?" She shoved her fist into his gut, not making a ripple in his stupid romance-novel abs. *Damn him for being irresistible.*

He grunted, held up his hands in capitulation. "I didn't put a spell on you. Just listen to me." He dropped his arms to his sides, rubbed his stomach, and backed away a step. "A black warlock by the name of Andre Charlemagne did. He's the world leader of the Black Tide, a group of long-dead and banished black warlocks rising from the ashes. The spell's breakable."

Willow clutched her churning middle. Her mind raced through her black warlock history. "How?"

"How he spelled you?"

"No, dumb shit." No sense in jabbing her foot in her mouth. One eye blink and he could kill her if he possessed Sage's magic and the magic of a black warlock. "You're a black warlock. How do you exist? Witches vanquished the lot of you years ago."

"Not all." A strange mix of sorrow and defeat shrouded his face, and his shoulders slumped a tad. "The Charlemagne and Ravenwood bloodlines were the strongest during the Witches and Warlocks War. We've managed to hold on to most of our magic."

"And enhance your magic by bonding the strongest witches?" *Holy crap on a cracker. Sage!* She may be in deep. Did her sister know what she'd done by bonding Evan? Willow had to warn her.

Evan's downcast eyes and silence provided her answer. Sage had no clue.

"What now?" she asked. "Mind if I use the bathroom before you bury me six feet under? I'd rather emergency personnel didn't see that I'd peed my pants before rigor mortis set in."

Evan smiled his wickedly sensuous smile, causing her daft hormones to stand at attention. Her life stood at risk and her stupid hormones didn't give a hoot.

"Willow, I'm not planning to off you. Or hurt you."

"Then what do you want from me?"

"Go use the bathroom." He scanned her tidy apartment, from the tiny, spotless kitchenette, to her desk and living area, painted in gradient shades of gray and purple. His gaze finally landed on her queen-sized bed on an elevated platform in the far corner, half hidden behind a koji screen, a slew of gray and purple pillows covering the variegated purple comforter.

"Then what?" She slipped out of her leather jacket, wanting to hang it on the hooks on the back of her door, but refusing to brush past his behemoth body. As if sensing her indecision, he snatched the jacket out of her hands and hung it up.

Cautiously, he spun back around. "I'll tell you everything."

"Why?" Willow stuck her left hand in her jeans pocket, stifling the urge to touch him.

"Because I want what you want." Evan reached out a hand and she flinched. He dropped his arm to his side, and his gaze raked her up from her feet to rest on her lips. "And because... I want you."

Willow's pulse leaped. *What the what?* She cocked her head to the side and glared at him. Why would a black warlock want anything to do with a poor excuse for a witch? Why would Evan want anything to do with her period? They barely knew each other. He already had Sage in his back pocket, so there was no need to get her on his side for whatever nefarious purposes he had in his pea brain. Silent, she stomped to the bathroom, slammed the door shut and locked it. She grabbed her small handgun stuffed under the sink behind a box of tampons. Since her magic sucked ass, the gun was her failsafe.

Staring at her pale reflection in the mirror, her fingers bit into the grip of the nine-millimeter. Leaving the safety on, she stuck the weapon in the rear band of her jeans. Not the greatest holding place for it, but it worked in a pinch. She peeled off her damp blouse and yanked on a long, baggy T-shirt, making sure it covered the gun. She texted Sage a 911, waited a few minutes. Nothing.

She pulled the band off her ponytail and brushed her hair around her face, hiding behind the wavy veil of auburn. Last, but not least, she flushed the toilet for show and left the compact bathroom, braced for another chapter in her night of horrors.

Evan had closed the blinds on her three windows and perched on the couch, waiting to kill, maim, or eat her. She shrugged. One or another, didn't matter. Death was the ultimate end at the hands of a black warlock. He gestured to her padded rattan chair, and she sat, once again mesmerized by his presence seeming to engulf the lion's share of the apartment's space. He was commanding and sexy, and had no right to turn her on the way he did. No man had ever made her want to strip to her birthday suit and have her way with him. No man had ever made her *want* so badly. Maybe Sage had a point. Willow glimpsed the bulge in his pants. A long, thick point to be exact. Willow needed to get laid. Or commit herself to a facility for the criminally horny.

Not with Evan, though. Not a warlock bonded to another witch. Especially not a black warlock. Rowing up shit creek sounded about right at the moment. One fragmented opening in her magic and mind, and a black warlock could seize control of all her magic. She'd lose it all sexing it up with him. No freaking way. Not with Evan Black Warlock Ravenwood. The sexiest warlock—black or not—she'd ever beheld.

"What do you mean you want what I want?" she asked, leaving his admission that he wanted *her* on the back burner. The idea terrorized her, and provided way too much fuel for her starving libido.

He rotated slightly on the sofa toward her, as comfortable sitting there as if he owned the place. "Simple. I don't want to be dominated by a witch. And I'm tired of hiding."

She clutched her neck. How did he know her main reason for not joining the coven beyond her lack of magic? Did he read minds? Who'd spilled her secrets? Or was he bluffing?

"Because you're a suck-up black warlock?" Her sarcasm refused to be caged. "Give me a break. I'm not stupid. If you possess your own magic, you don't need Sage or any other witch for their powers." She paused, finger on her bottom lip. "In fact, you haven't proven you hold any magic at all other than the electric flashes, whether Sage's or your own. You're bluff—"

The seams on her shirt ripped apart and the sleeves of her silky T-shirt slid sensuously down her arms, blew across the room and puddled on the floor. The pieces of material ignited in gold and amber flames. A sprinkle of sand materialized in the air, smothering the flames. Last, and certainly not least, a black rose sprouted from the ashes, and the flower morphed into purple—her favorite color. Magic swirled and eddied around her. Not a bare hint of sage scented the air.

Holy crap on a box of crackers. Evan exhibited three elements of magic: fire, air, and earth. No witch on earth carried more than two innate elements, which was über rare, and also meant no bonded warlock could carry three elements either.

Unless he was a black warlock.

Willow masked her shock, swallowed her terror.

"Satisfied?" Evan's rich baritone floated barely above a lethal whisper. The magic-created flower fell to the floor between them, laying there perfect and real.

"You... you hold three elements."

"Two. Air and earth. Fire is Sage's."

She scrunched her forehead. He'd masked Sage's witch-fire scent. How? Why? She massaged her forehead, smoothed out the lines, but it only increased her confusion and intrigue. What was his angle?

Come on, modern warlocks don't possess magic. "Are there more black warlocks or Black Tide in the Wilde Coven?"

"Not in the Wilde Coven. There are in other covens."

"What do you want from me?" Willow clutched her arms over her breasts, shivering from an onslaught of frigid air. "Why do you *want* me?" She held her breath, waiting for his answer. He certainly didn't want her puny, adolescent magic. Earthworms had more magic than she did.

"I want you as an equal partner." He smiled, his sincerity disconcerting her to the nth degree. "I also want to bring down the Black Tide."

Despite the horrifying predicament she'd landed in and the enormity of what he'd related, Willow burst out laughing. Blinking back tears, she said, "Seriously, dude. Even if you are a black warlock, you're barking up the wrong willow tree. A ten-year-old witch has more magic than me."

Evan scooted closer, forcing dry, earthy air to encage her without restricting her. "Not if I wake up your magic."

She studied Crimson fluttering up and down her right arm, black-tipped red wings lifting up and sinking onto her skin faster than Willow had ever seen. "There're hundreds of other powerful witches to do your dirty work. Heck, Sage would kill to take down a major warlock coven on her climb up her world-domination ladder."

"You're wrong. An untapped witch creates the best bond with a warlock. There's a reason your powers haven't awakened yet." Evan crouched beside her, his fingers trailing up her bare shoulder, traveling up her neck.

Willow froze. One wrong move and he could crush her windpipe with one hand. He hand-combed her thick, loose hair, leaving tingles across her scalp and his spicy, musk cologne infusing her senses. Crimson scurried off her arm, beat its wings frantically against her left breast, nearly causing her heart to clutch up. Her butterfly familiar was near ready to jump ship and entice Evan into Willow's holey web of magic. Willow had to forcibly exert mind control to press the butterfly tattoo into submission.

"I need *you*, Willow." He leaned toward her, his mouth

a hairsbreadth away from hers. "And I *want* you, Willow Wilde. As my witch, my partner, co-ruler of the Wilde Coven and the Ravenwoods, and..." He shrugged. "Eventually as my wife."

Chapter 5

Willow stared at him as if he'd turned into the Hulk, fluorescent green skin, torn clothes, and all. Evan's gut churned. Yet he refused to show her she affected him in a slew of ways, even though he couldn't hide his burn for her in his damn erection and the sparks dripping off his hand. Jet chirped in smug satisfaction for his ears only, and he clenched his fist to keep from smacking his familiar quiet.

He'd lost it and confessed too much. But the moment he saw her on the beach earlier, sensed her untapped magic in the witch circle, smelled her heavenly floral perfume overriding the sea air, he knew without a doubt he'd wait a lifetime for her and her alone. The kiss they'd shared during the summer, that strange and wonderful kiss, had kindled his desire for her, and he'd never lost sight of it. When Sage gifted Willow to him on a silver platter tonight, the spark exploded into flames, and he wanted nothing more than to take the beautiful and enchanting witch as his own.

After he'd sworn an oath never to get close to the

enemy. Or defy the leader of the Black Tide. Willow would get him killed. No, his desire for her would get him killed.

He'd gone too far, scared her. Disregarded his original intent and his unwavering orders. From Andre. For the black warlocks rising to power. He'd not only lost his mind, he tipped on the verge of losing his heart. What the hell was he doing? And why did he want her as his wife? Where the hell had *that* come from? If Andre found out, Evan would welcome death. One flick of Andre's finger and he'd find himself eviscerated first, then deader than a cadaver, no matter that Sage's formidable magic enhanced his own, making him a powerful adversary. Andre's perfect minion.

But Andre wanted Willow. Evan had no right to her in any way, shape, or form. He was following orders: trick Sage into bringing him into the coven, snag Willow, terminate his bond to Sage, and return to the Black Tide compound, prize in hand. Move on to his next task.

Then why did he feel like he'd die if he let Willow go? Die if he didn't kiss her luscious lips once again? Die if he sacrificed her to the darkest of the black warlocks?

Willow's hysterical laughter spun his mind back to the present.

"Wife? Crazy much? You're delusional if you think I'll marry *you*, or any warlock." She vaulted up and stomped to the door, opened it. "Get out. Take your marbles and return to your crypt or wherever you guys've holed up." She gripped her phone, texting someone, probably Sage.

Evan lunged, snatched the phone out of her grip, and stuck it in his front pocket. "Don't contact Sage yet." He towered above her and shut the door, holding it closed with the palm of his hand. "I've spelled you to keep Andre's slimy hands off you. If he gets an inkling his plan's gone up in smoke, he'll flip his shit. He knows where you live. And you don't want him showing up here. Your life will end in a shit shop." The scent of her perfume infused his senses.

A drowning sweet, womanly fragrance. A heaven he had no right to smell.

Seething, Willow glued herself to the wall between the door and a window, her distress staining bright spots of red on her pale cheeks. "You said you wouldn't hurt me. So holding me against my will is A-okay with your *high-ground* morals?" she mocked.

She licked her lips, a nervous and evocative move. His erection pushed against his jeans, forcing him to rein in his basest desires. *I can't do it, man. I'll be a dead man walking. Andre won't bat an eyelash sacrificing his best warlock if I defy him.*

"Hell, Willow." He held up his hands in surrender. "I'm trying to protect you. If you want to split, go. I won't stop you. Just know this. Once we're separated, my protection spell dissipates. You won't move five hundred feet before Andre swoops in and bags your ass. And you'll never escape him. *Never.* You'll become his unwilling consort. You'll destroy the Wilde Coven and eventually every other coven in the world. All on your head."

"*My* head!" she screeched, leaning forward as if to force her words upon him. "Are you for real? Been drinking lots of Kool-Aid lately?"

Her breasts strained against her T-shirt, the barest hint of her nipples thrusting out her shirt. Evan wanted to rip it off. Again, dead man walking.

"You walk, your choice," he said, his voice gruff and hesitant. If she walked out the door, he'd trip off the rails.

"Why doesn't Andre just snag me now?" She jabbed a tiny fist against his shoulder.

The contact of her skin against his shirt spread another swathe of heat across his chest. "It's not part of his plan. Unless I fail."

"Fail at what?"

"Ensuring your magic stays untapped. Bringing you to

him."

"As if that's gonna happen. He trust you?" She snorted and shoved past him to the center of her living area, kicked off her sneakers, rubbed her shoulder where she'd banged it against his upper arm.

"I can unlock your magic properly before he gets his hands on you. He'll break you if he tries." *Screw the crazy train. He had to risk it all for her. There's no going back now.*

Willow threw up her arms. "Well, of course. Why didn't you say so?" A sneer was overkill, but she met his grimace with one anyway.

When her right arm dropped behind her and arched around, he knew he'd find himself facing the barrel of a gun. He didn't flinch a muscle, didn't raise a hair of magic. "Shoot or don't. Your choice. Either you go along with my plan to save your ass and my own, or kill me. If we don't solve this now, he'll mow me down tomorrow. Then you'll never see the light of day again."

Her arm wobbled, and she gripped her wrist in her other hand, holding the gun steadier. A calm crept over her exquisite, porcelain skin. Her luscious bow lips parted, pert nose and emerald green eyes flared, all framed by her vibrant auburn hair. Hair he wanted spread over his chest while her mouth... *Shit. How'd it come to this.* Not like he didn't want her, but the situation was impossible.

There was one quick way to wake up her magic. One simple way to bind their magic and strengthen each other. One way to get the upper hand on the situation before it catapulted them both into the pits of hell.

A contemplative silence flooded their standoff. They never shifted their eyes off one another.

Finally, Willow asked, gnawing her bottom lip, "How can you wake my magic?"

"Bonding you," he said cautiously, truthfully, eyeing

the barrel aimed at his heart.

"Keep clinging to that raft." She snickered. "You're bonded to Sage. Only she can sever your bond."

"Not true. Not for a black warlock." An infinitesimal smut crawled over his skin. *Andre.* His shoulder muscles tightened painfully. Drawing forth his earth magic, he reinforced his faltering protection and banishing spell. His forehead creased in concentration as he whispered the words in his head. The longer he held the spell, the more intrigued and concerned Andre would get. Although not bonded to Andre, the man had put a tracking spell on Evan, on all his Black Tide minions.

She narrowed her exquisite emerald eyes. "You got fleas?"

"Strengthening my protection spell." He held out his hand. "I can't keep this up forever before crashing completely."

"How will you awaken my magic? How can you play that card if your magic can't protect me?"

"One quick and easy way." He rubbed his arm. There'd be nothing quick about it when they got down to business. "Please set the gun down, Willow."

"Break it down for me. Now." Willow advanced a step, cocked the hammer, the barrel mere inches from his heart.

"A spell and a heightened awareness of each other." He hedged, trying to protect his heart from splattering all over the wall behind him. "You need to be at your most vulnerable with your guard down."

"So... as in heightened awareness and vulnerability during sex?" Her mouth dropped open. "What kind of hillbilly warlock logic is that?"

"Yes, as in sex." He winced, waiting for a bullet to pierce his flesh, sympathy twinges shooting through his chest. "It's not the only way, but it's the fastest if we're into each other."

"Seriously, dude? You're so full of it. You just want to get in my pants. Wasn't. Born. Yesterday."

He winced. *Ouch.* "I won't deny I want you. What man wouldn't? You're gorgeous, smart, sexy. But it's the fastest and most successful way of awakening your power, by a black warlock, with all four elements present."

"Screw it out of me?" She laughed maniacally. He almost resented her disdain. "Like you even have the ability." Her face twisted comically and so cute, it served to feed his lust even more. Not even the threat of death dampened his stupid wayward lust. Even Jet fluttered excitedly up and down his chest, tickling and teasing his flesh.

"Willow." He grimaced, exhaled. "Your magic has been dribbling out. We saw it tonight. It's ripe for the taking and awakening. A coven spell of this magnitude can take days, even weeks with a circle of thirteen and may not be successful. Or we awaken you tonight. Just you and me. Fast and efficient."

"Just like that?"

"Am I so horrible to look at? To touch?"

"That's not the point, and you know it. I don't trust you. I don't trust the load of crap you're selling me. I don't trust any warlock. I sure as hell don't want to bond a warlock or rule over one. And we just met less than two freaking hours ago. I don't do one-night stands, let alone warlocks."

Then she didn't know he was the man she'd kissed last summer. He scrubbed his hand through his long, tangled hair. "We'll have equal magic. We'll be the first to break the bonds of witches' supremacy over warlocks. We'll make right the travesty the witches and warlocks have suffered since the Witches and Warlocks War."

Her arm dropped to her side, the gun aiming at the hardwood floor. She rubbed her temple for a few seconds. "I'm going to bed. I need to think." She waved the gun at him. "Don't come near me, or I swear I'll turn you into a sieve."

"Scout's honor." He gave her a two-fingered salute. "I'll crash on the couch." He let his protection spell slip into a jumbled layer of magic that would no longer trigger Andre's curiosity, but still keep a witch-eye on Willow. Andre knew Evan had to maintain certain spells to stay inconspicuous. The mix of air, fire, and earth magic might keep him alive another night. Might, being the operative word.

He hungered to touch Willow, wanted her in his arms, to soothe her confusion, and ensure he'd done the right thing. He wanted assurances he hadn't just signed his death warrant. The night had turned all kinds of crazy on him, but there was no flipping the lid on the insanity.

Evan had to have Willow as his own. If he *was* drinking the Kool-Aid, he wanted more.

He'd never met a witch, or any woman for that matter, who'd created such mayhem in his head and heart, not to mention the constant erection he'd suffered since her witch-water magic first kissed him on the beach in the drizzle that rained over them that night. She probably had no clue she'd caused that drizzle that only fell upon them. A frisson of her magic had shimmered over his skin, leaving behind a sheen of moisture, leaving him feeling that he belonged at her beck and call.

How the hell had a snip of a powerless witch changed the course of his destiny in a mere couple of hours? What would happen when he awakened her magic? Fear and desire barreled through him at breakneck speed on a collision course toward one another.

Before the weekend ended, he'd possess her in all ways. And he'd belong to her forever if she'd have him.

Chapter 6

The moon slanted luminescent stripes through Willow's blinds onto her comforter. She hated having Evan Ravenwood in her small apartment, guarding her. The last thing she ever thought she'd need was a guard, let alone a warlock. Damn that evil smut tailing her all over California. She'd asked for it, going to Sage for help. What did she expect? That Sage would let Willow walk away scot-free? *Nope.* Sage had a purpose in mind for Evan's presence, and it was more than keeping her little sister safe. It was Sage's way of keeping tabs on Willow and trying to sway her to join the coven.

A swathe of heat worked up from her toes, despite the cool temperature. Willow lay in bed, all too aware of the soft snoring emanating from Evan on her short sofa. His legs were bent at the knee, and his head was pillowed on the cushioned sofa arm. She almost felt sorry for him. Almost. Not enough to offer him her bed. He'd asked for the assignment, so he got what he got. At least she'd given him her best down pillow and a fluffy comforter. Not that he needed the comforter. Sage's—his—witch-fire gave him all the warmth he needed.

Insomnia setting in for the long haul, Willow swiped her covers aside and swung her legs over the side of the bed. A shiver worked over her bare legs, and her fitness tracker glowed three o'clock.

Evan snoozed onward, and she slunk quietly to her tiny closet. She pulled out her black leather pants and jacket, changed her mind and grabbed her black leather skirt and knee-high boots with blocky heels, heels to run in if she needed. The urge to leave some skin exposed surpassed her need for warmth. She needed air to touch her, needed it to temper the strange heat rising and abating within her. A fire she had a hard time naming. Was the heat part of Evan's protection spell, his derived power from Sage? The black smut? Who knew? But she also wanted some bodily protection from the external elements in the predawn of her stomping grounds.

Combing her fingers through her loose hair, she brushed it to the side and eased past Evan snoozing away like a good watch dog. A snort worked up from her throat and she choked it down.

The snick of the door closing set off a round of paranoia, and she gritted her teeth while she waited in the hall outside for thirty seconds. Evan slept onward, and she bolted.

She took off toward shore, cutting through the downtown village. In the early morning, everything was shuttered overnight, the streets she usually walked empty. She'd walked her route so many times during a full moon, she knew what streets to avoid to remain alone and anonymous. And safe. Even though she had her small handgun stuffed in the top of her left boot, she'd never needed it on the streets of the seaside town. Shadows seemed to follow and hide her even from the most curious person she ran across. The tailgating shadows were really a figment of her imagination, seeming so real at times, they may as well be the real deal.

Cool, crisp sea air circulated around her, filled with salt and brine and a tinge of rotting fish. Willow breathed it in deeply, filling her lungs to bursting before exhaling out the remnants of the old month. The full moon hung in the sky like a glorious beacon of hope, a reborn light to illuminate the new moon cycle.

Sometimes, she'd put on running shoes and run. This time, she wanted to absorb the night, the air, the earth beneath her feet, and the dampness from the ocean. The moon provided the tool in her personal ritual to diminish any negative energy built up over the month. As well as an aid to find her magic. Now that the clouds had mostly dissipated, maybe the moon might do the trick when it had so miserably failed her on the beach last night.

The cool air swamped Willow with adrenaline. She walked down one deserted street to a dark alley framing the moon on each side, lighting her path. The moon hung so low it seemed to swallow up the alley. Her heels softly clunked on the cobblestone street with each step closer to the orb in the sky. The beacon met the night and absorbed the black of the unlit alley, illuminating all but the darkest crevices.

Halting on the walkway between two three-story buildings to gather her bearings and to cleanse her mind, Willow closed her eyes. Soft classical music wafted out of an upper-level apartment over the retail space to her right. Lights remained off. Normally, the sound would distract her, but that night, it seemed to soothe her ragged edges. The scent of bread and pastries baking to her left filled her senses, tickled her empty stomach. Another early riser. Normalcy.

The low thud of hard-soled shoes sent Willow's eyes wide open in hyper-awareness. She spun toward the sound stemming behind her, peered into the dark, using the moon to illuminate her limited eyesight. Nothing. The footsteps halted. *It's not like I own the alley.* Even though she didn't own it, she was always on the lookout for trouble. She wasn't entirely stupid. The safety of the gun in her boot slayed a thread of panic. Many sessions at the gun range lent her even more security. Where her sisters relied on their magic, Willow had only her wits and a gun to rely upon.

She eased into the shadows of the building to her right. Moonlight slashed and bounced off a window above her head, and she moved closer to the building, her shoulder abutting the wall's rock façade. Hair bristled on the nape of her neck. She slipped the gun out of her boot and waited. The hard heft of the small weapon in her hand bolstered her nerves.

Slow footsteps grew louder, closer. Halted. Had they seen her? Fire sparked inside her. Fire? Or panicked heat? She couldn't tell. *Damn Evan's residual magic!* Witches hung on to residual magic for a short time after wielding it or being exposed to it. Willow had been exposed to a lot of magic in the last several hours. No wonder she had a hard time deciphering the embers inside her.

The footsteps sounded again, but this time they moved away from her. The footfall slowly faded away into nothing, and Willow breathed a sigh of relief. She waited a few moments to ensure the alley belonged to her and the night again before moving out of the shadows.

Walking at a fast clip down the pavers, the moon seemed to grow larger and swallow up the color around her, leaving an atmosphere of indigo ink coloring the buildings sandwiching her in.

Heat tingled in her right hand, burning the metal of the gun against her palm. She shifted the gun to her left hand and stuck it in her waistband, the tight leather giving little room. "Yeah, I know, stupid place for a gun," she muttered. "If they can do it in the movies, why not?" She snickered.

Another tingle of heat raced up the nape of her neck. Willow spun around, drilled through the moonlit night for another intruder.

Her water magic seemed to slosh around inside her, then disappeared as if the sun dried it up in the middle of the desert. *Par for the course.* But the fire magic seemed to expand until Willow wanted to rip off her clothes and dunk her fiery body in the Pacific Ocean, again.

"Willow. Willow Wilde," a man's singsong voice called from a few yards behind her.

She spun back around. The silhouette of a tall man stood centered in the alley. With the moonlight behind him, she couldn't make out his face or features, other than his bulky and very solid form. *Another one of Sage's warlocks? Was he shadowing me? Had he followed me from my apartment?* Breezy magic lifted the tips of his hair.

Annoyed, she slipped the gun out of her waistband. "I'm armed," she called out. "I suggest you keep on walking. I don't need another warlock on my ass tonight."

The man chuckled, a heavy throaty sound. "Need is relative."

"Relative or not, time to hit the road, Jack. Tell Sage to keep her warlocks away from me."

"She'll get the picture soon. When I get the chance. And that chance is coming sooner than you Wildes think, willowy Willow."

The man's words stopped Willow's heart for a second before it kicked into overdrive. *Is he a black warlock? Another one of Andre's minions? Goddess, save me from this nightmare.*

A strange fire inside her raged unimpeded by her mounting annoyance and a tinge of fear. In fact, her fear added an accelerant as if it blew on the dormant embers. *Strange-ass residual magic.* She couldn't waste time trying to get her witch-water to douse the heat. Not while she took care of this jerk.

A sudden gust of wind blew up and fluttered her sleek hair in all directions. She fought the urge to smooth down the flyaways. Nothing else moved in the alley, and she knew in that moment that the man channeled air magic. *Idiot warlock!*

"Knock it off," she growled out. "Who are you? Who's your witch?"

He chuckled. "If you only knew."

"Go back to your cave." Willow took a step forward, preparing to return home from her aborted trek. The moment her left foot hit the ground, a gale force wind pushed her against the side of the building, slammed her shoulder into the bricks. *Son of a witch's tit!* Pain lanced her shoulder, and she stumbled to right herself, hugging the wall for support. The wind continued to gust around her, her hair flying above her head, making it hard to breathe from the gale.

Bands of air enveloped her body, tying down both arms. She tried to lift her arm to aim the gun, but it was like the man had glued her arms to her sides. Another gust grabbed hold of her gun and flung it to the ground about twenty feet from where she stood.

The warlock approached, and his grinning features cleared as the moonlight illuminated him.

Willow didn't recognize the man sporting a light brown crew cut and pale luminous skin. Not the typical Santa Cruz beach-town tan, even in winter. His dark eyes seemed to glow preternaturally. Thin lips spread wide showing a bare hint of crooked white teeth, stretching laugh lines up to his chiseled cheekbones. Not unattractive, but not Sage's type. Not a Wilde warlock at all.

The wind died down, but the invisible air bands continued to hold her in place. The residual breeze accelerated the growing embers inside her. Maybe she could work with that since she'd lost her gun and her own magic had dried into spit.

With clacking teeth, she managed to grit out, "What coven do you belong to? What do you want from me?" Silence met her and she seethed. A spark grew inside her and dripped off her finger. *What the what?* He just stood there and grinned at her, tightening the bands of air, as if he planned to squeeze her to death. Her breathing became labored, and she had to force herself to calm down by focusing on that strange spark, that strange heat enveloping her, growing in intensity. Was it possible she possessed fire magic? Was that why her water magic never emerged properly? Did the two opposing elements fight for control within her? Excitement swamped her fear. *I can freaking work with that, too.*

The bands loosened, then tightened. He played with her now. Her hair lifted, swirled, fluttered down. Air toyed with her face, like a hand caressing her skin. She nearly growled at the man, instead shot him a feral glare.

Concentrating, shutting out the man and the world, Willow pulled the heat from her core into a ball the size of a dime. It flared and burned. Despite the breeze billowing around her, perspiration dotted her forehead. The ball expanded, and she focused on the moon to rid her of negativity, ignoring the jerk watching and grinning at her. Was he waiting for hell to ice up? It was like he wanted her to raise her magic.

Witch-fire filled her, dried up any water magic she possessed. She focused on the fire, calling it forth. It coalesced and sped up to expand the ball of fire until the magic exploded off the skin of her hand and the orb bounced on her open palm. Fire dripped from her like water. The warlock's wind blew the sparks around her, but only served to fan the flames brighter. Light flashed around her and melded with the moonlight, surrounding her in luminescence.

Willow's heart raced, and she grinned at the ball of fire. Positive it wasn't Sage's or even Evan's residual magic, she knew it belonged to her. It felt right. She felt right for the first time in her life. Finally. A witch. A real witch.

"What you gonna do with that, little girl?" Mr. Tall and Lanky interrupted her glorious moment, the moment she didn't want to share with this asshole. "Do you even know what to do with fire?"

"Wouldn't you like to find out?" The witch-fire inside her kept feeding the ball of light, keeping it strong and alive. Not a drop of water interfered with the fire. If she blasted the ball at him, his air would just knock it asunder or even scatter it. Could she form another one quick enough to do any damage? Only one way to find out.

In a blink of an eye, she hauled her arm back and tossed the fireball at him. Sure as shit, he waved an arm and swished the ball away where it splintered in a shower of sparks. Within seconds, she'd formed another fireball, bigger than the first. Sparks flew around her as his air magic tried to blow them away. Stronger, more intense and it took nothing from her hidden cache of magic. A lifetime of magic stored inside her and the doors had flung open. She didn't think she'd ever deplete the untapped supply. That is, if her water magic didn't douse it. A conundrum to figure out. Later. *After I blast this asshat to the moon.*

The fireball remained within her grasp despite the intensifying air trying to unseat her. Willow exerted extreme force of will to maintain her focus. She fought to push her swirling hair out of her face and keep an eye on mystery warlock. With a quick flick of her wrist, she tossed the fireball at him, but it clawed at the swirling air and fizzled into a shower of sparks.

Again, she grew another fireball, the magic sifting out of her like expelling air after every inhale.

The stranger's grin faltered. He advanced a step, tried to grow his air magic. It did nothing but try to whirl her into the sky. Anything not tied down in the alley spun in the air like a tornado. Miraculously, her magic grew the fireball to the size of a basketball. Conundrum time. The wind nailed her to the wall and there was no way she'd be able to raise her arm to throw the fireball at him. Once the magic left her, he'd just gust it away.

Flipping hair out of her face, she waited, grew her magic. Thought long and hard. Recited the only fire spell destined to prevail against wind magic. "So mote it be," she yelled and internally released her magic. The ball of fire cut through the air, barreled arrow straight at him, undiminished and stoked by his air. His magic wavered, and the wind began to die, the bands caging her fraying.

He had no time to move when the fireball struck him, slamming him to the ground. Out like a light. She cut ties to her magic to prevent him from burning to death. Murder never hit the top of her to-do list. But his zipped-up jacket began to burn across his chest.

"Shitshow, here I come." Willow pushed off the wall now that his magic had died completely and tugged off her jacket to douse the fire. By the time she shrugged it off, water dripped off her fingers. "Well, hell. Today's my witch birthday. Open the spout." She internally mumbled a water spell. "So mote it be," she muttered to a spurt of water spraying off her right hand. She waved her hand over the flames until she'd doused the fire, and stood over him, panting, exhausted and depleted. *Is he alive?* A shiver ran through her.

The obnoxious sounds of clapping sounded behind her,

and she swung around to her witness.

Evan Ravenwood.

Indignation arose and smothered her fear. "Are you following me? Did you put a tracking spell on me?"

"Didn't need to. Smelled your magic from your apartment." He walked toward her, the thud of his boots on the pavers grating on her last nerve. He picked up her strewn gun and handed it to her. After checking the safety, she shoved it back into her boot and put her jacket on.

"What do you mean you smelled my magic?" She bit her bottom lip, shook out her hand even though no magic or water dripped from it any longer. Her magic disappeared inside her as if it never existed, leaving her bereft.

He shrugged. "Sensed it is a better word. It permeated the area." He dragged the downed man against the building and into deep shadows. Sat him up and propped him against a drain pipe, making it look like the dude had passed out after a bender.

She blinked rapidly, spinning on her heels to see if any other witch or warlock had crawled out of the woodwork.

"Yep. We need to get the hell out of here before others descend." He gripped her upper arm. "Come on."

She shook off his hand, nodded her head at the downed man. "What about him? I want to know who he is and what he wants from me. Who bonded him?"

"He's not bonded to any *witch*." Evan grimaced, kicked a toe at the other warlock's leg. "He's one of Andre's top warlocks. Bounty hunter. Which means, Andre has all his dogs sniffing you out."

A swathe of shivers charged her, and she stumbled into Evan's strong body. He took her weight as if she were a feather, snuck his arm around her waist to steady her. She leaned into him. "I thought he trusted you to bring me back."

"Guess I messed up tonight. He's onto me."

She tossed up her hands. "Great. So how many of his warlocks do I need to hide from?"

"Few dozen." He steered her around and they began a fast clip toward her apartment, the moonglow guiding their steps.

Sounds arose from her left, and a door squeaked on its hinges, the click of the lock snapping a moment of base fear in her brain.

Cautious, she treaded forward. "How much did you see?"

"Enough to know you have both fire and water magic."

The idea sent a thrill through her chest. She stifled a groan. "How is that even possible?"

"How do you think? Sage has witch-fire and something else. Can't tell what it is." He said the words as if trying to get her to give up the goods. "Your family is strong in magic, like mine. Makes sense one or all of you carry multiple elements."

So Evan didn't know that her sister carried the mother of all magic, aether, a combination of all the elements. Good. He didn't need to know. No way did Sage let him sip magic out of her either. She controlled the magic she spoonfed her warlocks.

"Guess you don't need to awaken my magic now." Willow smirked, then a thread of disappointment wound through her. It's not like she'd have gone along with him, was it? *Holy goddess.* Did she have feelings for Evan? "My magic's alive and kicking."

"Guess again. You raised your magic out of fear. Now you need to awaken it completely *and* learn to master it. You need to keep both your elements from killing each other. Or yourself."

Chapter 7

A swampy silence reigned as Willow contemplated her potential magic. She'd heard of witches who had multiple elements of magic who didn't live to ripe old ages because their magic ultimately killed them. Willow scratched her head, patted down her flyaway hair. Yet Sage had no problem mastering her elements. Was it because Sage technically had aether, which is a combination of all elements?

"Aether works with all elements," Evan said as if reading her mind. "Don't accept Sage's learning experience as your own. You have two opposing elements which will fight tooth and nail for dominance."

"You just said you didn't know what magic she had."

"I suspected. You just confirmed. Her aether doesn't enhance the magic I derive from her or my own. She controls the magic she gives her warlocks well."

Willow stopped, and his arm dropped away from her. "Don't ever play me like that again," she gritted out between clenched teeth, more ticked at herself for giving up the goods on her sister.

"Willow," he breathed out her name. "I meant what I said earlier. We can do great things together. If we're honest with one another. I didn't mean to trap you into dropping family secrets. I suspected Sage had aether. Nothing else explained her particular breed of witch-fire, the intensity of it, the sharp edges of perfection. Aether as a whole doesn't belong to warlocks and it never will."

Willow heaved out the breath she held. "Aether merely enhances a witch's natural elements and makes Sage's elements work better together. It gives her a bit of all elements. The main element of aether is fire, which is why you wield fire."

"I figured." They resumed walking side by side. Evan kept his arms pinned to his sides and didn't attempt to touch her.

"Do you think I have aether?"

"Doubt it. Otherwise, your water and fire would work together without much effort."

"Who's to say they won't?"

"Which element do you feel the most?"

Her usual internal dampness had returned, not an ember in sight. "Water. What do you feel the most?"

"Sage's fire screws up my innate magic. But before she bonded me, I always felt my air the most. Earth is always there, but it grounds me, where air lifts me up."

Excitement swamped Willow. "Air makes you float."

"Pretty much." He chuckled. "It's an internal thing though. So do you feel your fire?"

"I didn't until this morning when I was threatened, for the most part. Maybe a bit on the beach." She tossed up her hands. "Sometimes I feel overly warm, and it ain't the female change."

"All hot and bothered?" His chuckle turned into a laugh.

Willow stopped, stared at his back. "Did you just

make a joke? Dude, you're not all one-dimensional, after all."

"I have my moments." He held out his hand. "Come on. Let's not linger." His hand enveloped hers, and she wanted the feel of his strength, the touch of his skin, the spark of desire flaring inside her. Not witch-fire. Good old-fashioned lust fire.

She recited a familiar spell to entice her witch-water out of hiding again, hoping to stem the tide of lust. *Nada.* It was as if she'd dreamed the whole incident, the fireball, the water springing from her fingers.

"Shoot," she muttered.

"What's wrong?" Evan's hand tightened around hers.

Heat enveloped her face. "Nothing. Just trying to work my magic."

"Like I said, your magic temporarily came alive due to your fear. Haven't you experienced tidbits of it before in moments of fear, extreme excitement or tension? If you want to master it, you need to awaken it fully." He loosened his grip, but didn't release her hand, and she eased closer to him.

The moon lit their path back to her apartment as dawn began to gray the sky and dull the stars twinkling through the moonglow.

Damn it all to hell. Now that she'd had a major taste of her magic. She wanted it, wanted it all. She couldn't even call one of her sisters or cousins to double-check if Evan could awaken her magic with his black spells. As much as she hated to fess up, Willow believed him, and she refused to betray his trust and spill his secret. Not now. Everything inside her screamed at her that he told the truth. And that he wanted her as much as she wanted him. That kiss at the party months ago had already sealed the deal. What did she have to lose sleeping with him? If nothing else, the sex will relax her, get her mind out of the gutter and screw her head on right to concentrate on awakening her magic.

Magic was so stinking close, bubbling at the gates of her soul! She'd do almost anything to unlock those gates.

They entered her dark apartment. Evan deadbolted the door and planted a warding spell on it, something he'd neglected earlier. She assumed the warding spell was for her benefit, as well as the protection spell to keep the Black Tide warlocks out. The warding spell kept evil away from her apartment, whereas, the protection spell protected her personally. Evan would know if she left the apartment again. Didn't matter. She didn't plan on going anywhere but to bed. To sleep. Sex could come later. Exhaustion had set up shop inside her, and if she didn't get a couple hours of deep sleep, she'd have no fight against Andre and his minions.

She stowed her gun under her pillow, tossed her jacket on the foot of the bed. Without a thought about exposing herself to Evan, she pulled off her boots and shimmied out of her skirt, leaving on her skintight T-shirt and thong panties. The bed welcomed her with open arms and she drifted off just as she realized Evan had stretched out on the other side of the bed. Far enough away to give her space, close enough for comfort.

$$C \star C \, C \star$$

Bees seemed to sting the inside of Willow's belly. The sinister being flirted with Crimson, forcing her familiar to seek shelter on the hollow of Willow's neck beneath her jaw. The attacking smudge spread throughout her body, laying waste to her pitiful magic.

The black spell had returned with a vengeance.

Willow fought the darkness, falling faster toward the inky power luring her to some unknown destination. She reached out, meeting invisible fire, and wrenched her seared hand to her chest. The invisible being tangled her thoughts, sliced through her dreams and replaced them with nightmares. She screamed from the invasion, spewed out ineffectual witch-water to douse the heat, flailing to escape the inky black void. Jolting upright, she quaked so hard, she awakened crying and nearly hyperventilating.

Real flesh and blood fingers alighted on her arm, and she jerked back, gripping her gun beneath her pillow. Heaving to catch her breath, her eyes flickered open.

Evan Ravenwood.

Tiny lines bracketed his eyes and swept across his forehead, showing concern on his handsome face. He perched on the edge of her bed, his hand hot and heavy on her thigh, having moved off her arm, comforting and eerily familiar. Protective.

The nightmare and pain ensnared her in its inescapable trap. An entity was pressing her body into a tortilla, smashing her bones and muscles, and shooting acid in her veins. And it wasn't the drug kind of acid.

"Willow? What's wrong?"

"The spell's back."

"Impossible. My protection spell's active."

"Active for who? It's not working on me."

He scrubbed his hand over his face. "Damn. Andre has penetrated my spell."

Pain stabbed the inside of Willow's skull, and she moaned, her eyes pleading for him to spell the pain away. Before she uttered a word, he'd wrapped his arms around her, laying her flat against his hard body entrenched on her bed as if he belonged there. Involuntarily, her mouth brushed his neck, and his cologne teased her senses, fogged her mind. The tail of Sage's white bonding owl, Snow, poked out from the collar of his T-shirt. Willow tugged down his neckband and pressed her fingertip to the sleeping bird tattoo. It proved Sage had bonded him.

Crimson came out of hiding and danced around her neck to rest on her shoulder. The butterfly's tittering excitement prickled her skin. Evan's innate air magic cooled the desire razing her insides where her own magic failed.

Bizarre to the nth degree. Crimson normally hates warlocks. More than she did. She usually had to stop her familiar from biting the coven warlocks if they moved too near. One poisonous bite from Crimson was enough to incapacitate a warlock for hours.

"Why isn't Snow angry at me for infringing upon Sage's *property?*"

Evan chuckled, his chest rumbling and bouncing her against his hard body. "We're bonded. Nothing more."

Willow snickered. "Right. You haven't played mattress tag with Sage?"

"Sage and Rafael are going exclusive. Apparently, she's not tapping her warlocks any longer. Nor have we *ever* slept together."

"She's talked exclusive for years. I'll believe it when I see it." The burning blackness within her had subsided to a dull roar. Life felt right in Evan's arms, and it puzzled the hell out of her. Earlier that morning she'd been willing to give him the benefit of the doubt, to have sex with him, to see where that furtive kiss months ago led them. After a few hours' sleep, nothing had changed. Except her desire had increased tenfold.

"Rafael has finally convinced her. They have something real." His finger landed beneath her chin. "Look at me." He craned her head back, and her gaze met his gray-blue pools of mystery. "I don't screw around. Sage knew that from the start."

Heat pooled between her legs, becoming a firestorm of need and want, obliterating Andre's black smudge. Evan eased away, insinuating air between Willow's body and the very hard evidence of his desire. Tentatively, playfully, she eased closer, stopping his movement. Whatever witchcraft he'd just practiced on her shoved a wedge between the black spell and her body, and turned on her hormone tap. *Damn. What is this man doing to me?*

Earlier, exhausted and battling an encroaching migraine, she'd conked out and let her guard fall to crap. Her instincts had ruled and dropped her walls. Evan hadn't taken advantage and Willow respected him for it. Maybe he was telling the truth. Maybe she should test him out, take him for a ride. Could he truly awaken her magic? Could he drive that black-ass spell into the pits of hell? Did he really possess magic equal to hers so she didn't have to become his master? If their so-called relationship traveled to that destination, that is. It was the thing she hated most about modern witches, one big reason she refused to join the coven. Even if she possessed magic worthy of the coven.

He kissed her mussed hair, his breath warm and soothing against her scalp. Willow both wanted out of his arms and didn't want to move. Talk about the conundrum going on inside her head and heart. She should fear him, fear what he represented and the intrusion upon her solitary life. But her mind refused to switch off from the length of his hard body against her soft curves. She desperately wanted to touch him skin to skin, and her fingers trembled from her need and indecision.

She'd never had sex with another man other than her former quasi-boyfriend, Michael. They weren't exclusive and it suited Willow to a T. Michael wanted more from her, but she had too much living to do before she committed herself to any man. Despite his best efforts, Michael wanted her, but she didn't feel an all-consuming fire for him. Not the fiery sensations Evan created inside her core, whether derived from Sage's witch-fire or from the man himself. And Michael wasn't a warlock.

"Willow, stop thinking." Evan's words shocked her.

Seriously, did he read minds?

His hand slipped down her stomach, sliding lower, and she realized he was touching her *bare* skin. She remembered she wore only a thong and T-shirt. Not even a bra. *Holy crap hitting the fan. A perfect storm.*

"I don't even know what you do, who you are." Willow fought a yearning she didn't understand for this man, trusting her sister that he wasn't a serial killer, or a serial magic stealer.

Evan laughed. "I'm studying computer engineering. Finishing my master's at Stanford."

Willow belted out a laugh, her mouth flapping open. "You're a *nerd* like a Silicon Valley nerd?"

He chuckled. "Well, you're going to be a shyster lawyer. Guess we're square."

A skittering awareness on her hip jolted a craving through her mangled mind, putting an end to learning more about him. Evan's hands angled toward her hips. Automatically, she curved tighter into his body, and a soul-wrenching desire cloaked her.

"Willowy Willow." His lips moved against her hair. "I want you." He touched her reverently, as though she were the powerful witch he'd envisioned ruling the world with him.

A flush suffused her chest as she fought her impulses to touch him intimately. Instead, she lifted her head and kissed him experimentally, a kiss she'd wanted since the moment she'd spied him on the beach last night and recalled the stolen kiss months ago. Willow's lips molded to his. The touch of his lips on hers kindled an inferno of need. A day's worth of stubble shadowed his jaw, and the rasp across her cheek kicked their first kiss into the forefront of her mind once again. She caressed his warm, tanned arm and rested her hands on the wide expanse of his powerful shoulders. His muscles spasmed beneath her fingers. A harsh sound climbed his throat, and he slanted his head, his tongue breaching her parted lips. Quivers formed at the base of her spine and raced along her nerve endings. Her tongue met his, and she tasted the lingering sweet tang of bourbon from her liquor stash.

Kissing him felt like fire, like air, water, and earthy. The rightness between them was insanity returning for a second helping. Had he spelled her? Hell, she didn't care. Let the spelling continue. Desperate for air, she freed her mouth and inhaled a shaky breath. Evan's hand slipped lower, feathering her thighs. The sizzling heat of his body spread through her T-shirt and ignited her insides. She moaned, aching for his fingers to continue exploring.

He kissed her neck and worked his way to her ear. The roughness of his whiskered jaw scraped across her skin before he tasted her lips again, his own both firm and soft. Her pulse quickened, and she moved enticingly against him. She was dying to feel more of him. And she didn't want him to stop his exquisite dance toward the open invitation her naughty parts were tossing out. Gasping, she almost lost it from the mere idea of him touching her where it counted.

Willow rucked up his T-shirt, moving slightly above him. An eagle tattoo spread across Evan's chest, and she jolted back from the fierceness of the bird's hulking wingspread.

"Whoa, dude. Familiar much?"

Evan stroked the bird's ruffling, wide-spread wings. "That's Jet. My coming-of-age familiar."

"The familiar that defines you? Same as a witch's familiar?"

"Did you expect any different? Warlocks and witches had the same powers at one time."

"How'd he come to be?" Willow tapped Jet's beak, and the bird pecked her finger lightly, testing or tasting her, she wasn't sure which. She eased closer to Evan, and Jet's soft wings evocatively brushed her nipples through her T-shirt.

"Full command of my magic came early at sixteen. I was still learning what it meant to be a black warlock in this world of witches and the Black Tide. I took hikes up to the peaks of the Santa Cruz hills to clear my head. One day I sat to think and watched Jet soar into the sky from the tops of the trees. He swooped and dove and put on a spectacular show. When he was done, he landed on my outstretched arm. We knew it was meant to be." He paused, kissed her forehead. "What about Crimson?"

She snickered, stroked his arm, feeling the corded muscle beneath his skin. "Despite my lack of magic, I still gained my familiar at eighteen. I guess Crimson sensed *something* in me. I was visiting my parents' graves at the cemetery in the spring. We'd planted all kinds of flowers around the family plot and many were in bloom. Crimson fluttered around them, then she kept landing on my head. I kept swatting her away, not really thinking that she might be a familiar. I nearly killed her with one swat but she returned and landed on my shoulder, began to burrow beneath the collar of my shirt. Then I knew. Shocked me, you know, since I didn't have my magic. I always thought Crimson was a gift from my mother."

Silence reigned, and her familiar cooed in her unique way. Evan kissed her again, inciting a renewed need.

The eagle's wings rose and sank beneath Evan's skin, fluttering slightly against her. She flicked her tongue over his left nipple and it pebbled instantly, ruffling Jet's feathers against her lips. Low groans indicated Evan's approval, and she continued to trail kisses over his chest and throat. His spicy, musk scent infused her mouth, fed her flames. Fervor sparked in her chest as his fingers skimmed across her shoulder, lower to caress the rounded side of her breast.

His other hand reached lower, and the exquisite sensation jolted her against him. Evan continued a sensuous dance on her sensitive flesh. She closed her eyes, reveling in the sweet vibrations tipping her toward the edge.

Evan nudged up her chin, and she forced her eyelids open. Passion swamped his sapphire-darkened eyes. Doubt flashed behind the desire, and his hands ceased moving.

She exhaled an exasperated huff and thrust her hips against his hand, giving him her assent. Eyes wide with acceptance, his mouth descended again, devouring hers in a short but possessive kiss.

She was defenseless to stop this warlock from infringing upon her body in all the ways she used to hate, but now craved.

He loosened his hold on her chin, and her head bowed again. "Look at me!" he demanded, shooting an unexpected thrill through Willow's chest.

His eyes had gone wild, like the midnight sky. Evan continued his pleasurable assault on her hyperaware skin. Masterfully slowing, teasing, tormenting.

"Goddess alive, Evan, don't you dare stop again." She combed his shoulder-length dark hair, sexy silk spilling across her pillow, still giving him a rugged handsomeness.

"Go over for me." His mouth found hers again. When he nibbled her bottom lip, she parted her mouth, and he slicked his tongue over her lips. This time, he took her invitation and speared his tongue inside her mouth, mimicking the dance of his fingers. Hypnotized by his kiss, lust clouded her mind. Tremors of arousal rolled down her thighs.

Willow wanted to rip off her T-shirt and rub her skin against Evan's slick body, but she dreaded moving. She dreaded the reality of the bald eagle softly cawing and ruffling its feathers on his chest. Something she'd have to confront. Afterward. Later. Eventually.

Their kiss deepened, and his finger dance sped up. A never-experienced pain-pleasure built within her. She wanted it to stop, needed it to find an outlet, and never wanted it to cease.

"Oh goddess," she moaned, biting his upper arm to muffle her cries of pleasure. Waves crested and peaked inside her.

"Fly for me, little butterfly," Evan rasped out as spasms overtook her and her spine arched. He tore his mouth off hers, and she saw herself reflected in his wide, sharp eyes. Jet's wings tickled her face. A tempest of air ascended and swirled about them, blowing through their hair. Crimson flew off her and danced on Evan's shoulder. Passion melted her magic into molten drops throughout her entire being.

She slumped on top of him, sated in a way she possessed no words to describe. Crimson flew onto her arm, trailed by a tiny eagle, both dissolving onto her skin, frolicking happily together. Shocked, she focused her blurry vision on Evan's intense face, the unnatural light radiating from his eyes, his untamed magic. They rolled onto their sides, facing each other, and his mouth landed on hers, capturing the breath of her passion.

Evan had given her his bonding familiar. *What kind of sick joke is this?* Modern-day warlocks didn't possess familiars! Witches gave their multiple bonding familiars to any old warlock and even multiple warlocks, for protection, sometimes sex, and sometimes because they had a connection of sorts. Yet warlocks of centuries ago gave their one bonding familiar to only the witch they expected to spend forever with. To the witch he intended to bond for life. To the witch he'd lost his heart to. *Holy hell. I'm in deep.*

Chapter 8

Pale light laid soft stripes across Willow's bed. Across Evan's dead asleep body on the other side of the bed. She checked her phone. *Nada.* The clock read four in the afternoon. They had slept the day away. Practicing witchcraft came with a payment in terms of depletion and exhaustion.

Letting her so-called enemy drive her body to new heights of bliss, exacted additional payment. Before they fell asleep, Evan had planted a platonic kiss on her forehead and rolled over to give her badly needed space. She didn't even have to tell him she needed the distance. He'd sensed it. It'd been *never* since a man had brought her so much gratification without going all the way.

Confusion had set up shop in her mind, her traitorous body, and her heart. It still plagued her. The dinging of her cell phone, discarded on her pillow, flung reality back into the day.

Magic fizzed just under her skin, residual witch-fire either Evan had left behind or she created. His tiny bald eagle familiar, a monochrome tattoo on her skin, moved silent, stealthy on her right upper arm. Crimson rested on her right shoulder blade. Restless and watchful, cooing disconcertedly at the bird, unsure of the eagle's position in Willow's life.

She shut down the phone before it woke Evan and let the call roll to voicemail. Probably Sage checking in. She texted her sister, "I'm alive," and Sage texted back, "Good. Check in later." No way in hell did she plan to tell the Wilde Coven leader about the new magic teasing every inch of her body.

"Ugh," she whispered and flung the covers aside, slipped on a pair of leggings from the stack of clean clothes on her dresser. Tiny sparks dripped from her fingers, witch-fire raring to go. Not one drop of mist interfered with the fire. Maybe she didn't really have water magic.

"The witch-water will come back."

She spun around to find Evan eyeballing her every move, his gray-blue eyes wide with a promise that shot blooms of heat to her cheeks. "You saw that?"

"Pent-up magic. It's dominating your water."

"But my witch-water never really made a full-blown appearance until last night."

Evan shoved off the bed and stood, scratching the dark scruff on his jaw. "Doesn't mean it hadn't been there overshadowing the witch-fire. You've always thought you had water magic, right?"

Heading toward the bathroom to brush the fuzz off her teeth, she replied, "I only suspected. It was that nebulous." Heat bloomed in her middle that had nothing to do with magic. She had to escape his allure before she pushed him back onto her bed and practiced her sex magic on him. *If only.* She nearly slammed the door shut.

"Is Andre plaguing you?" he called.

"Nope."

"Good. My protection spell's still working," he said

slowly.

She opened the door a crack, toothbrush poised to get busy. "You sound skeptical. Don't freaking tell me you doubted your protection spell. What good are you guarding me if that's the case?" She stuck the brush in her mouth before she layered on more sarcasm. At this point in the game, she honestly liked his presence and didn't want to tick him off.

"Andre keeps his abilities close to the vest. I suspect he might have the same aether magic as Sage because of his strength. Unlike Sage, the mere fact that he's a black warlock means whatever magic abilities he has is cataclysmically evil. It's just the nature of a black warlock."

Willow stopped brushing and spit in the sink. "Including you?"

Evan's face reddened. "Black magic's rising, Willow. All black warlocks possess the ability to weave and cast black magic spells."

"And to bond any witch?"

"Yes. And bond a witch."

Willow tossed her toothbrush aside and hugged her arms across her chest. "I still don't understand why Andre wants me, an untapped witch."

Evan approached, and she moved out of the bathroom so they could trade places. He gargled mouthwash, taking his time with the task as if contemplating the right answer. Finally, he turned back to her, scrubbed his hands through the snarls in his hair. "He obviously sensed something in you. Your power, your family's power. An untapped witch is easier to train in the arts of black magic. You don't have prior prejudices and biases."

Willow seemed to shrink in on herself. "So I'll be easy to bend to his will," she nearly whispered. She lifted her head, straightened her spine as if someone shoved a steel rod up its length. "He can go fuck himself before he gets his paws on me."

Evan stepped forward, gripped her hand gently in his, tugged her closer. Not touching, but close enough to feel his body heat. Immediately, the fire in her awakened and sparks tickled where her flesh met his in their clasped hands and radiated up her arm.

"That's why we need time before he comes for you. Once your magic is fully accessible, it'll be harder for him to control you, especially if you have two elements. Better still if you completely controlled your magic, but that will take too long."

"And that's why *you* want to awaken my magic with your black spell?"

"Willow. I'm not taking advantage of you. It's for your own benefit and safety to have complete access to your magic ASAP." His thumb rubbed her hand, soothing the fire popping off her skin. "This is all you."

She smirked. "It's my reaction to you."

"My air fans your fire," he whispered. "They react well together."

She pressed her hand to his chest, as if to hold him back, but in reality, she wanted the contact. "No, *you* fan my fire." Lifting on her toes, she pressed a quick kiss to his mouth. He tried to deepen the kiss, but she backed away, drew her hand out of his. "I want to practice my magic before you use your evil black spells on me. After my alley toss-up, maybe I can do this on my own. It's so close, I can taste it."

He leaned forward as if to press his words into her brain. "My way is better." Evan feathered his forefinger down her cheek, wrapped a lock of her hair in his fist.

"Maybe." Heat sparked in her southern region. "But I need to do this on my own. You have no idea how long I've waited, how hard I've tried. If I fail, we'll do it your way."

She spun around, felt the yank of her hair as he

untangled his hand, then faced him again. Poking a finger in his shoulder, she said, "If you betray me, it'll be the last thing you do. Because if I don't kill you, Sage will."

"I know," he said simply, confident.

"Then let's begin." Willow pushed furniture out of the center of her living room where she'd already formed a witch's circle beneath her rug.

"Food, coffee first? You'll work better fueled and fed."

"Shower, then fuel."

After a hot, then cold shower to wash Evan and her night off her skin and a skimpy omelet that matched the contents of her fridge that Evan served up, Willow was ready to get the show on the road.

She licked her lips, sucked down the dregs of her caffeinated ambrosia. "Where did you learn to cook? And make coffee?" Her gaze lingered on the empty pot sitting on the counter. She'd rather drink coffee made from fresh beans over a plastic pod any day. But she'd reached her limit. After all, it was almost dinnertime. She dropped the cup in her open dishwasher and shut it.

Evan wiped down the counter. "Anyone can make an omelet, and coffee's only as good as the beans you buy."

"And he's modest too." Playfully, she whacked the dish towel across his butt, before tossing it on the counter. "So what's for dinner?" she teased.

He laughed. "Don't think I can squeeze out a meal from the two tomatoes and one container of yogurt in your fridge. Ever hear of a grocery store?"

"Haha. You're a riot. I would've hit the store today if it wasn't for..." She wanded her arm around her. "This. You." The moment the last two words rolled out of her mouth, magic attacked Willow, a slow, growing flare of fire creeping up her back, crawling over her shoulders. She sagged against the counter, wrapped her arms around her midriff. The black smut was so intense and smothering, tears sprang to her eyes.

"Willow?" In one fluid step, Evan stood in front of her, his body dominating her personal bubble. His presence didn't stop the flames of evil, though.

"The black magic's back."

"Damn. Andre has found a way through my protection spell." Evan wrapped an arm around her waist, and she rested her weight against him instead of the cold, hard granite. "How bad?" His gaze swung to the center of her apartment, landed on the rectangular rug between her sofa and small dinette set. "Circle under the rug?"

She nodded and pushed away from him, slogged to the middle of the room. "Will it help?"

"Better than nothing. I can ward the circle with you in it." He quickly rolled up and tossed the rug aside. "Candles, salt?"

"End table storage." She reached the storage cube before he did and pulled out the cannister of salt and four elemental-colored candles. When Evan tried to take the salt from her, she halted his hand on the bag. "No. I have to do it."

He held up his hands in capitulation. "A black warlock has the same abilities to set a circle as modern witches."

"Doesn't matter. I need to do this. I need to know it'll work." Her glare cut him in two. Despite not having much access to her innate magic, she still knew how to work rudimentary spells not requiring innate magic, still knew how to create a circle.

Evan nodded, and Willow quickly sprinkled the salt around the chalk circle, set the pillar candles down at each point to represent the four elements of earth, air, water, and fire. Another wave of black magic swept up her chest and she gasped at the intensity of heat.

Visualizing a white light circling from the North/Earth, she quickly walked clockwise to each quarter and associated element: East/Air, South/Fire, West/Water. As she called upon each element's magic and protection, she lit the candle and walked the perimeter of the circle until she'd ignited each pillar. She mentally envisioned the circle forming an orb around her. "The circle is cast. So it is."

The heat dissipated and the fire fled. She straightened her spine, bolstered her spirits, and turned to Evan. "What do you need from me?"

"Just stay in the circle. I'll ward it."

"Will he know you've thwarted him?" She sat in the center of the circle, already feeling the pain ease.

"Yes. But I think he's playing with you... and me."

"Call him, get him to back off."

"That'll just provoke him." Evan held up his hand to forestall further talk. "Let me recite the spell."

Evan closed his eyes, weaved his fingers in the air as he recited his warding spell. "So mote it be."

Eyes closed, Willow slumped forward and took ten deep breaths, exhaling each slowly.

She lifted her head and gazed at him standing outside the circle, lines of strain furrowing his brow. "What if he shows up?"

"He won't risk leaving his compound. He rarely does. He's easily detected by witches. Plus, he won't risk that you don't have a quorum of witches here that might trap him."

Willow leaned back and rested her weight on her arms. "I can't stay here forever."

Evan tossed a pillow in her lap. "Sure you can. I can toss food to you." She whacked his leg with the pillow and he laughed, sobered. "Sorry, crude humor." He sat on the sofa arm. "Look, I'll text him and tell him I've got you under control, that you were hurt yesterday and are recuperating. He wants you strong, fresh when you come to him. I believe he'll bide his time, control his warlocks."

"Do it." She rose to her full height, a new energy invigorating her now that the black smut had taken a hike. "Meanwhile, I'm practicing my magic."

"In a warded circle?" Evan's fingers stopped on his cell phone, his eyes raking her face.

She shrugged. "The circle will just contain the magic."

"Exactly. What if it's too much magic and bounces back on you?"

She rolled her eyes. "Really? Too much? Have you seen me?"

"As a matter of fact. Recently. In an alley," he ground out.

She flapped her right hand in a dismissive gesture and moved to the center of the six-foot circle. "Let me do me and you do you." Closing her eyes, she shut Evan and the outside out of her small world.

Willow concentrated on her water magic, calling forth the element she'd mostly felt all her life, the cool balm that'd always been present within her. Opening her eyes, she faced the blue candle representing water, recited a spell to call forth a mist. Nothing. Evan eagle-eyed her the whole time. Almost ready to catch her if she fell or failed. Frustration set up a thumping in her skull. She spun toward the kitchen faucet and tried one of her tricks to get water to run out of the faucet without touching the handles. *Nada.* She closed her eyes again, concentrated harder, but there wasn't an extra drop of witch-water to be had inside her, let alone doing her bidding outside her body.

She stamped her foot on the hardwood floor. "It's not working."

"Water?"

"Yeah."

"Try fire. It may be drying out your witch-water."

A light bulb moment flickered on in her head. "Damn.

Didn't think about that. I may never get used to having two elements."

"I have no doubt that you'll conquer both. After your exhibition this morning, your power's on the verge of emerging for good." Evan set his phone on the dinette table and stood outside the circle, careful not to touch the ring of salt and splinter the line protecting her. He blew out the candle representing fire. "Try re-lighting it."

"Hey!" She stamped her foot, cringing when pain radiated up her knee.

"You don't need the candles to maintain the protection circle."

Willow hung her head, scrubbed her face with her fingers. "Argh. I'm hopeless at witchcraft."

"Don't sell yourself short. You'll be stronger than Sage."

"Not if that asshole bags me."

"Over my dead body." He reached for her hand, and she let him grip it.

"You would die for me?" The smirk traversing her face was probably overkill, but so what.

"Not what I said," he chuckled, squeezed her hand and let go. "But I would. I'd rather die for you than Andre or his clan."

Willow let his comment slide. For now. Too much to unpack when she needed to crack the code on her magic lock, or block, or whatever denoted her magical glitch.

"Oh. Kay. Back away. Don't want to roast you with all my power." She waved him away. He didn't budge. "Move, don't move. Don't blame me." A smile pulled her lips up at the corners.

Willow concentrated on locating fire inside her. With her mind's eye, she searched and searched for a spark, a tinder, something, to no avail.

The only heat she suffered was a flush of frustration

over her face. Once again, she found Evan staring at her. Any other man and she'd feel like she was a fat, juicy fish in a fish bowl. But somehow, his scrutiny didn't bother her. In fact, she liked it. She liked his message, if he told the truth. She liked that she might have worth to the coven above and beyond the normal witchling under Sage's dominance and power.

"I can't find my fire. Witch-water is probably dousing it."

Evan scratched the scruff on his chin. "What did you do early this morning?"

"It was just there. Came to me without much thought."

"Before or after you were threatened?"

"I felt both before walking down the alley." Willow sat in the middle of the circle, crisscrossed her legs, propped her elbows on her legs, chin in her hands. Exhaustion threatened, or maybe it was plain frustration and indignation. "Then he attacked me with air, and I gained fire control after that."

"Maybe the protection circle and my ward *are* killing your abilities."

"Did Andre respond to your text? What did he say? Can I afford to leave the circle?"

"He seems okay with you recuperating"—he did air quotes—"for a couple days as long as I keep in contact with him and play my part."

"Why does he trust you so much?"

"He'll kill my family one by one if I betray him."

Willow's head jerked back. "What? You didn't tell me that."

Eyes watering, he shrugged. "It's his way. Everyone's expendable."

The thought that Willow may be the source of death upon the Ravenwood family set her bowels gurgling. "What happens if you don't bring me to him? Who dies first?"

"I sent a nine-one-one text to my family. They're on alert, ready to fight. They know the stakes."

"And the prize?" She thumped her fist to her chest.

"And the prize." He held out his hand to her, and she grasped it. Evan tugged her out of the circle and into his arms, holding her close to his chest. Warmth and security encased her. "A prize that can change everything." He paused. "We can fix your problem in a simple way."

She snickered, pulled out of his arms. "Sex doesn't solve everything."

"It will this, unless you don't desire me and loathe every second." He snagged his phone off the table, thumbed through it and handed it to her. "Here's the black magic spell."

In black and white the "ritual" to tap into her innate magic, release it, and also bond her to a black warlock stared her in the face. Combining their magic until their bond was broken. She thumbed through the pages of the digitized ancient spell book, all authentic black warlock spells.

Handing the phone back, she backed away from him, swallowed hard, swept her gaze up and down his magnificent body. Landed her gaze on his exhausted, pale face. A chill worked its way around her and she shivered. "I need to try this on my own, before… before," she croaked out.

"Willow." He sighed. "Any other time, any other circumstances, I'd encourage you to do this on your own. But—"

She held up a hand to forestall him. "I know. I know." Muttering curses, she stomped away from him, as far from the circle as she could get in her small studio. "Just give me space for a while."

"Fine." He moved over to the door. "I'll do my job and stand guard." Evan almost spat the words out.

No matter what she tried, thought, or felt in the next hour, her magic had abandoned her. Not a drop of witch-water, not an ember of fire. Frustrated and exhausted, she flung herself on her bed, arm over her eyes. "Fuck me screaming," she muttered to herself.

"Your wish is my command," Evan said, his voice a smooth whisper, too near, too enticing.

Willow groaned in mock annoyance. "Shut it, Evan."

"Are you ready to call it?"

Willow slitted her eyes enough to see him sitting in the chair next to her bed. Grinning. *One of the worst days of my witch life and the black-ass warlock is grinning.* "You're loving this?"

Suddenly, his grin dissipated and pain etched lines around his eyes. "The witch world is depending on us to right a century-old wrong. My family's life depends upon the magic you and I can merge and create. Your family and coven will depend upon our joined magic."

Willow pulled herself up, settled her back against her padded headboard. "I still don't get it. Why me?"

"I told you, you're of less value to Andre once your magic awakens. He'll target another untapped witch. And probably enslave you in his witch pool for later use."

"Love. Ly. That'll just piss him off and help destroy us all anyways."

"Not if we have the upper hand. My family's been planning a coup like this for a decade. We'll get Sage quickly on board. We have enough power between the Wilde Coven and the Ravenwoods to take Andre down, with some insider help. He falls, the Black Tide falls."

Willow banged her head against the headboard, ignoring the stabbing pain through her skull. "It all sounds so nebulous. I just can't wrap my head around it."

Evan left the chair and slid onto the bed. He stretched out beside her, his long length so close, she immediately felt the heat of him. She wanted to drown herself in his warmth. Fighting the urge, she put an inch or two of space between them.

Turning toward him, she sucked in her breath at his beauty. *Goddess alive, why me?* She reached out to touch his biceps, licking her lips at the strength beneath her fingertips. *Why not me?*

Need for him cloaked her, and there was no escaping the heat between them. No escaping the course of action she knew in her heart she had to take.

Chapter 9

It wasn't that Willow didn't want to make out with Evan, or heck, go all the way just to shut up her demanding body. It just seemed like such a dire step and one of which she'd never heard. Now she'd read the spell from a credible source and it may be irrefutable. Before moving forward though, she had one item to clear up.

Night had descended, and Willow's smart lights flicked on in her living area, casting shadows on the abandoned witch's circle, glittering on the salt crystals like diamonds.

Willow snuggled into Evan's side, hiding her face against his chest. His T-shirt was well worn and soft. He wrapped his arm around her and pulled her even closer.

"It was you during Summer Solstice," she whispered.

"The kiss?" Laughter laced his voice.

"You know I was drunk off my ass. I thought you were—"

"Someone else? Yeah, I already figured that out."

"Why didn't you say anything?" Finally, she lifted her head to peer into his face. His pale tiredness had been replaced by an anticipatory blush.

"You didn't say anything either."

"Because I didn't know until I pieced it all together the next morning. By then, I was mortified."

"Hoping I'd forgotten? Or was too smashed myself?"

"Yeah. Something like that."

"Does it matter now?"

"It does. Because it was the best kiss of my life." She hung her head, picked at invisible lint on his T-shirt, unable to believe she'd just confessed a deep secret.

"Ditto. That kiss connected us. It's never left my mind." He squeezed her closer to him.

"That kiss and the fact that you didn't take advantage of me at that time or later, has helped solidify my trust in you."

"Well, hell. A kiss is all it took?" He chuckled. "I can do it again."

She playfully pinched his arm. "I just wanted to get that on the table. I was having a bad night, didn't care what warlock I was kissing. I just wanted something tangible to take home after seeing all that magic at the gathering. Alcohol got the better of my good judgement."

"Doesn't it always?" Evan sighed heavily. "Is it that bad not having your magic?"

"It's fucking torture."

"Then let me end your pain," he whispered and kissed the top of her head, his breath ruffling her hair.

Her need for him grew, and his heat nearly set her on fire.

Evan rubbed his hand up and down her arm, leaving it tingling with a spray of sparks chasing his hands. Her head sagged onto his chest, and his free hand moved to her thigh, his touch intoxicating. She reached to unzip his jeans.

"Careful." Evan sucked in a breath.

Trailing kisses up her neck and nibbling her earlobes, he cupped her right breast beneath her T-shirt, massaging, scorching.

Maybe she should've stopped. But her whole body took on an awareness she'd never believed possible. She shimmied out of her leggings and tossed them at the foot of the bed. Back in Evan's arms, she brushed light kisses across his lips, his cheek, and down to his neck. He quivered against her, tipped her chin up and captured her mouth. Evan kissed her like he was drowning and she was his lifeboat.

An unfamiliar and demanding need no man had ever satisfied simmered deep in her core, furiously reaching the boiling point. Lips already tender and swollen, Willow broke the exquisite kiss and peered into his lust-reddened face. "Evan, I want you, despite the magic awakening." He'd ensnared her in his web as much as hers had entangled him. He'd become her air.

He growled low in his throat and rasped out, "I've wanted this since the moment I laid eyes on you at Summer Solstice." His lips nipped at hers.

The idea of being the coveted prize of this man in her arms seemed to crack open the doors to her fire magic. It sizzled inside her. Water quickly doused it before she combusted. The boiling water did nothing to drench her desire, though.

The wantonness and freedom she felt for the first time quickened her pulse. If this was what it took to wake up her magic, bring it. Screw the consequences. She helped him strip off his shirt, and then tugged his pants down, exposing his strong tanned legs and so much more. Willow slipped to her knees between his legs and slowly planted kisses down his torso. He stopped her with a gentle hand on her head.

"I just want to be clear, Willow. I'll recite the spell to

end your torture. The spell will also bond us. But you won't master me like the coven's warlocks. We'll be equals unlike anything you've seen in our lifetime. Do you understand? Do you accept me?"

She nodded, two quick jerks of her head. Stalling, she said, "Let me taste you first." *Mental forehead smack.* Her words made it sound like he was a lollipop. One she wanted to devour down to—and including—the stick.

Willow pressed a kiss to his belly button. Despite her anxiety and hoping to ease it, she teased his navel, swooping her tongue in and out. His flesh rippled beneath her tongue. He growled, his hand tangling in her hair. Emboldened, she inched lower, her hair skimming over his inflamed skin, blanketing her hand in fiery silk.

Evan's spine arched, his hands finding purchase on her head. "Ahhh, *shitshitshit.*"

Crimson and the little eagle fluttered down her arms, moving from Willow to Evan and back again, flapping to the tune of their hearts beating.

Willow continued her slow tease until Evan stopped her just shy of losing it.

Arms trembling, he heaved her into his embrace, locking her body on top of his. Meeting her lips, he molded his mouth to hers demandingly, possessive. Slowing, his seductive kiss left her faint, and he continued to plant smoldering kisses from her mouth to the tip of her ear. The rough scrape of beard stubble across her neck was almost more than her sensitive skin could bear.

"You about killed me, beautiful." His fingers brushed over her rear, kindling the fire breaching her skin. A fine mist of water tempered it. "Imagine how you'll feel after we awaken your magic." He lifted her damp forefinger and sucked it into his mouth. "You're already coming alive. Imagine sharing our magic in a way unknown in this century."

The sincerity of his words deluged her. "I'm coming alive for you."

"No. Your magic is awakening for *you*." Evan claimed another searing kiss. Dizziness overwhelmed her as their kisses grew frantic, and he began to rock her world to the depths of her soul.

Her hips moved urgently against him. She needed him, or she'd die. Evan let her up for a quick breath of air before his mouth claimed hers again, tongues dueling. He cupped her butt, his fingers tenderly massaging. She was lost. Completely, unutterably lost. How could she forego what he promised? Or what Crimson and her gut told her was right? Crimson could have killed him by now with bite after bite of poison if her familiar felt Willow was in danger.

And he'd given her his precious eagle familiar. Historically, black warlocks didn't freely give up their bonding familiar—if they had one—before bonding with a witch. Mind blowing. *Black warlock enchantment?*

Willow lifted above him, caught his eyes in an intense gaze. "I need you now."

His shoulders coiled rigidly beneath her fingers. Evan gently raised her off him, leaving her floundering on her messy bed. "Wait," he ground out, frustration forcing past the raw lust reddening his face. "Are you really ready for this, for me?"

Willow's lust dulled as reality whacked her upside the head. Moving closer, she rested her head on his chest, breathing raggedly, forcing her lungs to catch up to her heartbeat.

He couldn't wake her magic. She couldn't bind him. Not until Sage renounced her tie to him and broke their bond. One night of fantastic sex was the only item on the menu. The rest had to come later. *Later? Holy hell.* She was thinking of *later*. With a warlock. A black warlock to boot. It all smacked of insanity.

But he was a *man*, one who'd already seeped beneath her skin, seizing a part of her she never imagined she'd give to any man. Plus, there was that whole waking-the-magic-to-save-her-ass-from-Andre thing.

"Why did you give me your eagle?" She kissed the tattoo tail of Jet on his damp arm. The bird lay flat, silent, completely absorbed onto his skin.

"Crazy as this sounds, you're it for me. I knew it the second I sensed you last night, despite my mission. Rebel knew too. I barely kept him restrained, he kept trying to fly to you." Rebel flew up Willow's arm, chasing Crimson across her shoulders, fire and air tickling her skin. Evan's air magic and her fire magic. They played well together. As well as her soft planes fit to the solid planes of his body.

"Does Sage know you have familiars?"

"I kept them hidden. If she did, she would've known my true nature and would've buried me." He laughed wryly.

As if summoning her sister, Willow's phone rang from the front pocket of Evan's jeans on the floor beside the bed. She froze, Evan stilled.

"Answer." He kissed her head, snagged the phone and handed it to her. "I won't keep you from telling Sage whatever you need. I need you to trust me."

Reluctantly, Willow left the comfort of Evan's embrace, and their entwined magic glittered in the air like tiny stars. She seized his pants off the floor and stabbed on her phone.

"Sage, 'bout time you called." She held Evan's jeans across her front torso, covering her nakedness as she escaped to the bathroom for privacy. One glance in the mirror proved her mouth was kiss-swollen and her hair a snarled rat's nest. She sat on the closed toilet seat.

"What's the nine-one-one?" Sage yawned loudly.

"Did you and Evan ever have sex?"

Sage laughed. "Don't be a Silly Sally. I don't share. Besides, Rafael and I are going exclusive. I've given all my other warlocks free rein to roam." Willow exhaled a sigh of relief. Sage continued, "Is he as good as his large pocket pal makes me believe he is?"

"Shut up." Willow banged her forehead on the vanity. "We haven't gone all the way."

Sage laughed. "Love, he's good for you. I want you in the coven. I want you following our ways, which includes you mastering a warlock. I can't think of a better one for you than Evan."

"Do you know Andre Charlemagne?" Willow forced the subject off her sex life. Dead crickets hit the line. "Sage?"

"Where did you hear that name?" Sage's tone deepened, icy, lethal.

"What about the Black Tide?"

"Where, Willow?" Sage demanded. Rafael mumbled in the background, no doubt alerted to trouble by Sage's tone.

"Names I overheard on the beach earlier," she lied. "Are black warlocks really alive? Are they threatening the coven?"

Sage exhaled heavily, tapping her fingernails on the phone. "Yes, on both accounts."

"Do you think a black warlock spelled me? Is that why you sent Evan?"

"Evan?" She snorted. "He has nothing to do with black warlocks or black magic. I sent him because his power rivals Rafael's." Sage punched her on mute for a few seconds before continuing, "I didn't want to give up all the goods, but, yes, we believe you were spelled by a black warlock. I've found no other source for what's affecting you."

"By Andre?"

"I've spent the night researching how to break the spell. If Andre spelled you, this can be dangerous. I didn't want to worry you." She paused. "Willow, are you okay? Is Evan still there?"

Renewed apprehension surged through Willow, tightening her chest muscles painfully. "I'm okay. Yeah, he's here. No threats," she lied again to set her sister at ease, and to keep Evan's secret. Why she felt the need to hide his secrets was a brain drain. Yet her instincts warned her she needed to protect him against the coven. If Sage discovered he was a black warlock, she'd draw and quarter him witch-style.

Willow wanted him alive, wanted him at her side. His smoldering gaze, his sensuous touch, and his spicy scent had irretrievably awakened her body. He wasn't far from awakening her heart for the first time ever, let alone unshackling her magic. She refused to allow him to die until they'd played this through.

"Are you close to finding a vanquishing spell?" Willow asked.

"I need to fine-tune it. I'll call you in the morning."

Willow beat the phone against her head. "Okay."

"You'll keep Evan with you? Please, Willow. You have to."

"Promise." Willow clicked off. Evan blocked the doorway. She had no clue how long he'd stood there in all his fantastic naked glory.

He pulled her off the toilet seat and into his embrace. She dropped his pants and the phone clattered onto the vanity. She wrapped her arms around his waist.

"She doesn't know you're a black warlock. She knows about Andre, though," Willow said.

"I won't lie to you. Not now."

"But you would've before—"

"Maybe." Evan tightened his arms around her and rested his chin on her head. "Come back to bed." His growly entreaty reignited the bonfire in her body. "You don't need her to break the spell. I can do it with our magic together."

He turned her on like no man, from his penetrating gaze, his gentle touch, his electric kisses. She wanted all of him. For one night. Or forever. One day at a time.

Willow lifted on her toes and kissed him. He groaned in her mouth and slid his tongue between her parted lips. The kiss demanded, and her hand splayed over his left nipple, over his chirping and vibrating familiar.

Breaking the sexy-as-sin kiss, he scooped her up. Evan flicked her bedside light on, and she noticed he'd turned all the other lights off. She arched her eyebrows.

"I want to see every inch of your beautiful body all night long."

Chapter 10

Willow's auburn hair fanned silky flames over the pillow. Evan's feverish gaze raked the length of her naked body, an amber slant of lamp light marking his trail.

Was he crazy thinking about uprooting everything after one night of potentially epic sex? He'd never experienced the intense craving he felt for Willow for any other woman. How'd he get so lucky to land such a sizzling hot witch? For a night, or longer if he had his way. He was damned sure not giving her up to Andre. Not to any man. Or warlock. *I'm totally screwed.* He hoped awakening Willow's magic gave him a way out of handing her over to Andre on a silver platter. No way could he do that to her. Not now. Not ever.

A smile found its way through Willow's mask of uncertainty. Eager and alive, her smile was enough to drive a man insane if he didn't taste that sinfulness on her lips. Snagging his arm around her waist, he hauled her onto his lap against the warmth of his skin. He tasted her kiss-ripened lips, her moan echoing through his body.

Wantonly, she rubbed her breasts against his bare chest and his desire ignited another notch. Jet and Rebel moved to the back of his shoulders, out of his way, granting his approval. Willow skated her tongue up his neck, teasing his earlobe, trailing across his fevered skin to brush tiny kisses on his mouth. Letting her take control, he withheld from devouring her mouth again. She kissed the flesh between his ear and throat, and his pulse accelerated from the heat of her mouth.

The pleasure seemed natural, and Evan's body responded to the memory of Willow's lips pressed to his. It wasn't only her body and her kisses that had kept her at the forefront of his thoughts since he'd first met her at Summer Solstice. He'd liked her warmth, her sarcastic sense of humor, the way she'd made him think of a better future, and more recently, the way her eyes seemed to look at no one but him.

Pulling away, he eased her onto the mattress and rested between her thighs. He feathered one hand along her peach-smooth leg up to her thigh. Lips pressed to her neck, he smoothed his other hand across the slope of her breasts, inhaling her intoxicating scent. *And everything nice. Goddess, I'm sunk.*

Her lips parted, and he brushed his mouth over them. His hand slid into her hair, drawing Willow closer to him. Soft and gentle at first, his kiss possessed her. He speared his tongue inside her inviting warmth and explored languorously, meeting her tongue in a stormy dance. Never-felt power whispered in his blood. Willow's untapped magic. Water *and* fire. Shock slammed him. He knew the makeup of Sage's fire magic too well. The fire he felt at that moment was white-hot, intense, and middle-earth deep. Way more intense than Sage's aether-tainted fire.

Realizing the power he held in his arms, Evan

tightened his hold on Willow, as if protecting that power from escaping. Linking her arms around his neck, her short blue fingernails bit into his shoulders. He reveled in the pain, wanted more as long as she inflicted it. Exploring her body with his hands, he kneaded the soft flesh of her ass before moving onward. Focusing on her scent, a garden of flowers in bloom, tinged in vanilla, he fought for every iota of control.

Amber lamplight dappled her pale skin, and he traced the dots with his fingers. She trembled, her sinful gaze not sliding from his. They shared another kiss, tender and hungry at once, sending currents of sensations prickling over him.

Evan feared his inability to resist Willow. It maddened and beguiled him at once. "I've never wanted another woman the way I want you. It's crazy."

"How can this be?" She raked her fingernails across his scalp, and he burned hotter for her. Willow's heart drummed against his chest in perfect sync with his. "Can we just enjoy each other this one night?"

"I don't know if I can walk away from you after tonight."

"Maybe I won't let you," she teased, then sobered. "Why didn't you say anything when I called you Nathan last summer?"

His face flushed even more. "Because I wanted to be Nathan."

"Oh. Nathan's nobody, by the way."

"I know." Evan nipped her shoulder. "A lower-ranking warlock's not for you. Not now."

Willow only somewhat bristled at his words, evidenced by her fleeting frown. "So why expose yourself now? Why not then?"

"Morally, I can't keep doing this. The Ravenwoods have fought Andre in secret for too long. The time is ripe for an overthrow. Witches and warlocks inside and outside your coven know change is upon us. Shutting him down is the first step. Well, after we wake your magic, that is."

"Why am I so special? Surely there're other untapped witches out in the world."

"Andre has followed your coven since he was old enough to kill with magic. He knew your parents in college, knew how powerful they were together. And he's kept tabs on you and your sisters all your lives. When your powers didn't manifest normally, he believed it was because you had multiple powers and that your magic fought each other for dominance. It happens before you learn to master your elements and prevent them from overpowering each other. He also believed you were meant for a higher power, and your magic wouldn't awaken until you were ready to fulfill your destiny."

She snorted. "Suppose he thinks he's the *higher power.*"

"He thinks he's all that and more." He braced himself on the bed to support his weight, his fingers dancing across her sensitive parts. "You want me to stop?"

Willow sucked in a breath. "You'll stop when I command you." A smile played at the corners of her lips.

She combed her fingers through the hair at the nape of his neck, and goose bumps crept over his skin in the wake of her delicate touch. He lost himself in the depth of the power she wielded, the longing for him and more he witnessed in her eyes. The power she held over him, the beginning of his total undoing.

Unable to stop kissing her, his mouth captured hers in a long, slow seduction. Willow parted her lips, and he slipped his tongue between them, moving slow around hers, enjoying her sweetness, tasting their destiny. Their kiss became fierce and demanding when she drove her tongue inside his mouth, sweeping it along the edge of his inner mouth, then lashed his tongue in a frenzied battle.

Evan about lost it, and he jerked up, gasping for air. Willow's breasts heaved, and her hands curled at her sides. Her lips were red and swollen.

"Don't you dare stop," she pleaded.

Evan kissed the flowery-sweet skin between her breasts, flicking his tongue over each nipple.

"Evan. Evan, your tongue is so made of awesome," she rasped out. "Maybe you're that higher power." She snorted again.

Chuckling, he inclined his head to watch her. Her eyes glazed over and rosy spots stained her cheeks. The sweet floral, vanilla scent of her washed over him and he breathed it in deep. "Fly for me, little butterfly." An unfamiliar emotion hitched his heart for a second before he continued pleasuring her.

Willow chanted his name, held on to his hair, a searing pain spurring him on.

Suddenly, his internal magic shield cracked, and her witch-water poured into him and mated with his magic for the briefest moment. *What the hell?*

Willow shouted, "Evan! Evan! Oh, no. No. No." She convulsed violently against him as her orgasm hooked her.

Their bonding familiars, Crimson and Rebel, moved across her abdomen, flying lower, taunting him. He sat back, easing the pressure.

Her eyelids fluttered open. "Inside me, Evan, or I swear I'll kill you, *master* warlock."

"Yes, mistress." He grinned, enjoying the role of co-masters. Something he'd always wanted despite the role he'd reluctantly been forced to choose in the Black Tide, the role he'd sacrificed in the Wilde Coven. He flung the thoughts out of his head and buried himself deep inside her.

Returning his mind and body to satisfying Willow, he

kissed her, halting his mind's trip to darker territory he'd rather not think about.

All of a sudden, magic breached his head. Willow's magic. Molten fire. Not water this time. *Damn. It's true. A fire and water witch.* She was the perfect match to his earth and air magic. Mind tangled, he stopped moving.

Words of the ancient binding spell came unbidden to him. A flickering cord of lightning whipped over their head as he whispered the words. Mentally, he grasped the cord, forming nine knots to weave the spell. He couldn't halt the spell or the knots from forming. The words were no longer unbidden, but he felt it was the right thing to do. Twice he tied off the final knot and it unraveled each time. Frustrated, he mentally tried again and whispered the final invocation, "By knot of nine, what's done is mine." The knotted cord lashed the air wildly until it dissipated onto his bare skin, a slight sting as it dissolved, and he completed the spell. The last knot burned through his arm like a branding iron. Something seemed off. But he had no time to think about it. All he could concentrate on was Willow and the reaction of her body against his.

Eyes hooded and lost in pleasure, Willow never noticed the spell, and he quickly began moving within her again. He needed it, needed to distract the shitshow he was about to unleash. Willow's pleasure and magic tumbled exquisitely within his head and body. He gave in to it and unraveled completely.

Twin fluttering rushed over his arm, quivering beneath his skin, and settled over his heart. Her fire and water magic flirted with his air and earth, creating a tsunami inside him. The meld of magic subsided as his elements dominated the co-mingled magic. But a strange taint seemed to linger, and a frisson of fear raced up his back. *Had Andre managed to breach the bonding spell?* He couldn't shake off a feeling of doom.

Panting, he sank his weight onto Willow, holding her in his embrace, worrying she'd disappear if he released her. Tickles chased over his shoulder, across his arm, and Snow flew away and vanished.

Son of a witch. He'd broken his bond to Sage. He should've remembered that would happen. A warlock can't bond two witches at once. Willow screwed up his mind, his concentration. He shook his head, unable to breathe or think of anything except her body writhing and panting beneath his, as they came out of their sex-crazed cocoon. His nerve endings kindled and his flesh roasted where their slick skin made contact. Her witch-water couldn't keep up with cooling them down. His air magic only fanned the flames, and he pulled back on the magic.

"Damn, Willow. You. About. Killed. Me." He nuzzled her neck, and a tear cascaded down her cheek and rolled to his mouth. Still lodged in her warmth, he rolled them onto their sides in a more comfortable position before his dead weight crushed her. "What's wrong?"

"That... oh, holy hell. That was insane. I've never—"

Evan took her mouth in a demanding kiss, and she accepted him with a greedy groan. Their kiss became slow and languorous. A kiss to drown in. A kiss to solidify a future for them. Together? *How crazy-ass is that?*

Willow whimpered against his mouth, and he broke free, seeking more air.

After a few moments lying in each other's arms, regulating their hearts' return to reality, Willow opened her eyes. The desire he witnessed on her face destroyed him.

"Weird, I can't feel my magic like I thought I would. But I feel different." She kissed him lightly on the mouth and drew back a little, frowning at his upper chest, a startled expression reforming her face. "Crimson? Rebel?"

He followed her gaze to her familiar and his bonding

eagle securely ensconced on his shoulder. Shock immobilized him, and his spine stiffened.

"Crimson, come back. I command you." Willow tugged the sheet over her breasts as she scrambled to sit back on her heels. "I didn't give you permission to leave."

The red butterfly didn't budge. "Crimson!" Crimson flew behind Evan's neck. Rebel followed.

A long silence ensued and her forehead scrunched in concentration. Face a mask of confusion, she pressed her fingers to her heart, her middle, and her forehead as if feeling for something missing. Wide horrified eyes landed on his face. "You lying piece of shit. You stole my magic!"

Chapter 11

A chill scraped across Willow's shoulders. Evan had betrayed her. Worst of all, her gut betrayed her. She'd also let her hormones beat her into submission for the first time, and it landed her in the worst jam imaginable. She'd let go of everything she'd believed in for the best sex she'd likely experience, with no strings attached. If she didn't want them. *With my bum luck, I may as well be pregnant with an STD if birth control and a condom hadn't protected me.*

Their actions that night traveled way beyond the normal guilt experienced from a one-night hookup. A witch without her magic, no matter how ineffective, was like a witch losing her identity, her sight and hearing, her touch and taste. And she'd lost her magic to the worst kind of enemy. *Manipulative, soul-sucking, black warlock traitor.*

Fruitlessly searching inside herself for an iota of magic, left her bereft and lonely. Like he'd ripped her heart out of her chest, leaving behind a gaping hole of nothing. Trying again and again to raise fire, water, anything, she nearly crumbled into a mass of skin and bones.

Evan climbed off the bed, bunching the sheet around his waist. "It's not what you think. I didn't steal your magic."

"You bound it or something. You went way beyond awakening my magic and bonding me." Willow let out an angry screech. She dove for the gun hidden between the bed and nightstand, hoisted it up, letting the comforter fall to the floor as she leveled the weapon at his groin. "If I can't have my magic, no one will." She'd lose her magic for good if she killed him before he released it back to her. Nothing less than he deserved. But losing her magic for good would ruin her, despite her lame inability to access it fully.

He raised no magic or finger to protect himself against her. Willow dragged in a slightly relieved breath. At least he wasn't trying to use her magic against her, if he even had the ability.

"I summoned the spell to open your magic like we agreed. Not to steal your magic. Something went ass-end up. You've got to believe me." He held up his right hand, holding the sheet over his so-called manhood with his left. "Put the gun down and let's figure it out."

"Figure out what a lying bastard you are? Sure, try me." Another hole decimated Willow's core, leaving her an empty vessel, frigid and dead. She'd never realized how much her tiny bit of magic was a part of her, how much she wanted it, needed it. How blind and stupid did she have to be? Even if her magic was insignificant, she'd inwardly hoped someday she'd become a full witch and join a reformed and modern coven.

In that moment, she was dead to the Wilde witches and their coven. Dead period. She tripped the hammer on the gun, her hand faltering as silent sobs shook her shoulders. "I fucking hate you." Not as much as she hated herself for falling for him and his machinations.

"Willow, sweetheart—"

She strengthened her grip on the gun, steadied her arm. "Don't call me sweetheart," she gritted out between clenched teeth. "You don't have the right."

He kept talking as though he hadn't just chopped her life into pieces for the ravens to feed on. "Andre can't use you if you're magicless. You're useless to him."

"Oh, so you think *you* can use me? Who elected you puppet master?"

"Nothing's changed from what I told you earlier. Black warlocks are weavers. I wove a protection spell, then a binding spell to contain your magic before unleashing it on you fully." He slowly let his arm drop to his side. "My protection spell slipped and the binding spell took over and didn't release your magic. It happened in the heat of the moment." Evan's eyes glimmered. "Fuck. I messed up."

"A weaver?" Willow's jaw dropped. *Today's witches can barely weave a physical cord, let alone an intangible cord.*

Evan shook his shoulders. "Old magic has stayed with the remaining black warlock bloodlines throughout the years."

The implications were boundless if what Evan said was truth. Later. She'd need to expose his abilities to Sage later. At the moment, other things bogged down her mind, her psyche, her heart. "Why didn't you ask my permission to bind my magic?" Scalding tears cascaded down her cheeks. She hated her vulnerability. *Ass-wipe warlock.*

"It wasn't exactly queued up on my mind. I mean, hell, didn't you feel what was going on between us? I was gone. I couldn't just stop and hold a convo with you."

Willow conceded a bit, not that she believed him. He had his motives, and was still a black warlock working for the enemy. But she hated that she would've given him anything for the sensations and pleasure of him inside her, on her tongue, slicked on her skin, the sound of his voice and breath in her ear.

Evan took a step toward her.

"If you move, I'll turn you into a eunuch." She swished the gun in a chopping motion.

"I haven't raised a lick of magic against you, have I?"

"Right. Not since you *stole* my magic." Despite her sarcasm, the arm holding the gun wilted to her side. Eyes trained on him, she snatched up his T-shirt and slipped it on. It hung down to her thighs. His captivating spicy, musk scent surrounded her, and she breathed him in deeply, wishing to scrub away her uncertainty and the cold fear slithering in her belly.

Before her mind moved on to another crazy-town conversation, the front door blew open, flames shooting off the frame three feet into the room. A deafening feline roar preceded the biggest, blackest panther inside her apartment. Willow screamed and hopped on the bed, aiming the gun across the room. The bullet fired wild, blistering a hole in an abstract oil painting across the living room.

"Well met, my pretties." A slight, wiry man followed the panther into the apartment, dripping arrogance, his smile ten degrees of ice.

Jerk alert. Andre Charlemagne. The man from her spelled dreams. Long black hair hung to his waist. A white goatee on his angular chin contrasted sharply against his familiar dark aquiline face, high cheekbones, and blade nose. The green of his eyes sparkled unnaturally. No taller than five-nine, his presence permeated her entire apartment. Water and earth magic radiated off him, and the fire scalding her door was spelled versus innate magic. The air reeked of a brimstone potion. She'd recognize the scent anywhere after spending her childhood smelling her sister Aspen practicing her alchemy.

With a soundless order, Andre stopped the panther from advancing, and he parked himself beside the humongous beast.

"Willow Wilde, it's my greatest pleasure to meet you." Hiding his scowl, he turned to Evan. "And you, Ravenwood. She wasn't for you to sample before you delivered her to me."

"Andre," Evan greeted. "Screwing the witch got me what I needed from her. Subdued her. She was on the cusp of awakening her magic. Now she can't use magic against you. She's all yours."

Willow's jaw dropped, and she lifted the gun again. Andre flicked his wrist, and a wave of murky water formed and rushed her and Evan, washing them against her back wall. Sputtering, Willow slid down the wall as the wave carried the gun into a whirlpool forming on the floor, swirling the weapon out of reach. Willow coughed out water and scrambled to gain her feet. Evan staggered against the wall on the other side of her bed, holding a soaked pillow over his limp dick.

Andre stared at Willow's breasts molding her soaked T-shirt. "Evan, my boy. It's not nice to fool Father Nature." He waggled his fingers, and the panther moved toward Evan, slowly licking its chops as if Evan was prey to an ancient hunger. "Do you think me stupid? This girl has no magic. I feel her magic on you. I smell her all over you."

"You can kiss my ass," Willow said, diverting and stalling him. "You're not going to pimp me out." Snark best served in a jam.

Once Snow returned to Sage, she'd know the shit had hit the fan. She should arrive any moment. *Right?* Willow beseeched the goddess for help, praying her sister arrived soon and equipped to take down the most powerful warlock this side of the galaxy. In his case, looks were very deceiving, until you took a gander at his familiar stalking Evan. History revealed that only the most foreboding warlocks and witches had such powerful feline familiars.

"Ah, sweetling, you know what I want. I want a return to the old ways. I want revenge against the witches who destroyed us. Simply, I want the power of an untapped witch. There's much I can do with your power, with you bonded to me. You wield the two elements I don't possess innately. I'll be the first warlock in the world to wield all four elements."

Two elements? Just like Evan. Damn, maybe *she* was a black warlock disguised as a witch with her supposed two elements. *Snort.* "Dude, you've got your history wrong." Willow crossed her arms over her breasts, madly wishing her entire life wasn't soaking wet. "Witches destroyed the ancient warlocks when they defended themselves from the warlocks trying to destroy us. Now you blame us for what *you* caused? Float the fuck off."

"If that belief keeps you awake at night, who am I to put you to sleep?" Andre laughed, a snively, wheezing sound.

"Read the Witches and Warlocks Historical Compendium lately?"

"Words can be deceiving."

His familiar sniffed at Evan, its mouth and long fangs so close to Evan's groin Willow experienced sympathy twinges. Evan stiffened, not a muscle moving.

"My boy, you had no directives to take the chit's magic, or to engage in relations. Tsk. Tsk." Andre tapped his finger on his bottom lip. "Do you want to choose your punishment, or shall I?" Without visible movement as if he teleported, Andre stood next to the panther again. His hand alighted on the feline's head, scratching the animal behind the ear. The panther growled and advanced another step toward Evan.

"Hold on, Andre. Nothing in my contract says I'm not allowed to sample the merchandise, as long as I deliver. You said you weren't interested in her as a sex toy."

"True. And that may prolong your life, enough time to give the witch her magic back and remove your paltry protection spell. Did you think me such an ignoramus that I didn't know you had spelled her against me?" Andre laughed again. The panther bared its lethal fangs at Evan, its mouth turned up in the feline equivalent of a smirk. "And you, witch. Did you think I wouldn't know about your little murder of one of my best warlocks in the alley?"

Evan lifted the fingers of his right hand to signal the panther from approaching closer. Andre nodded and the panther stopped. "I was keeping her coven out of the picture. Trying to hide her from their magic, and get her to accept my protection. Exactly what you asked me to do. They attempted to vanquish your spell last night, and ended up putting both protection and tracking spells on her. The alley thing was an unfortunate incident. I managed to subdue her before she caused more damage."

Evan lied to Andre. Sage hadn't plunked a tracking spell on her. Had Evan told the truth about stealing her magic to protect her? Had one night of fantastic sex caused him to defy his master and endanger his own life? Muddled webs knitted in Willow's Swiss cheese brain. Disconcerted and shivering, she desperately wanted to believe in Evan.

One night had changed everything. *Evan* had changed everything. Willow didn't know how to move beyond the night with or without him, if she escaped Mr. Blowhole and lived to tell about it, that is.

Andre flicked his hand. The panther backed away a step and rested on its haunches at Andre's left side. "An interesting concept. I do believe you may be telling the truth. You swore a blood oath to abide by my rules. I simply cannot understand you breaking your oath for a mere untapped and outcast witch." He waved his arm dismissively at Willow. "Or was she exquisite in bed?"

Evan shrugged. "I've had better. She satisfied a dry

spell."

"Eat shit and die, Evan!" Willow gasped, despite the inflection in his tone triggering her wariness. She shoved her hand through her soaked hair, scratching her scalp, spurring her brain cells into action. *Welcome to my crap carnival.*

"Mind if I put some dry clothes on?" she asked, mind revolving around the gun the water washed toward her closet door, covered by her waterlogged comforter.

"By all means." Andre smiled at her. "A dress if you own one. Preferably red to match your beautiful mane. Once you're mine, I'll buy you a whole new wardrobe befitting the Dark Queen of Warlocks."

"You're just a gift that keeps on giving," she muttered. Ever so slowly, Willow eased to her closet beside her bed. Andre's eyes seared into her backside until Evan drew the warlock's attention off her.

"What now, Andre? As far as I'm concerned, our mission hasn't changed."

"Oh, but you're wrong, my young stud. You'll return Willow's magic in order for me to seize it."

"I'll have to tap her again." Evan's words sliced through Willow's heart. "Magic stolen must be returned in kind."

Tears threatened. No one had ever kissed her the way Evan had, a soulful kiss flooded with his all, awakening something unnamed deep inside her. *Was she merely a hit and run? Another notch on his bedpost? A prize to give away?*

Willow yanked on a loose purple sweater over her wet T-shirt and a pair of jeans. Asshole Andre could take his red dress and screw off. She peered over her shoulder. The black warlock and his panther had their sights glued on Evan, contemplating his dire words. The last thing Willow wanted was to screw Benedict Evan again. Unfortunately, it was also what she wanted more than anything, other than her magic stuffing her hollows again and Crimson flitting on her skin in the awareness she'd loved since her familiar had come to life. Her bonding familiar butterfly, Rosebud, remained flat on her upper arm, having never arisen from its state of stasis. The bond between her and Evan hadn't been completed and won't until Rosebud moved off her to Evan. Evan was correct in that his spells had backfired. He couldn't even do a stupid bonding spell right. Acid gurgled up her gut, and she wanted to upchuck the entire ghastly night all over Andre and Evan.

"A conundrum, eh, Slink?" Andre patted the panther on its black head. "Using an archaic spell to trick the victim in a state of epic arousal." Andre scratched the panther between its ears as the feline growled its assent. "A farewell fuck? Hmmm." Andre canted his head, as if contemplating whether to grant an act of rape or not. A part of Willow definitely felt violated by Evan's betrayal.

Willow wanted to go medieval on them both, rip their hearts out, and serve them up to the panther for a snack. Yet a niggling doubt kept tangling her mind. Was Evan trying to protect her? Was he stalling Andre, knowing Sage wasn't too far away? A tiny thrill raced across her chest, chasing the idea of a warlock taking equal control. She almost forgave Evan his transgression in stealing her magic. *Damn it.* She needed concrete answers. Frustration ground her back teeth together.

"Andre, the Ravenwoods have pledged fealty to you. We're allied. You know I'd never break our oath for the sake of mere sex."

Nailing her peripheral vision on Andre, Willow slyly dug her foot in the drenched comforter, seeking the gun. She didn't know if it'd fire or not. A mist of magic draped the room, and she suspected he'd erected a protective cloaking spell. Could she even bang him down through the spell?

Subtly sweeping her foot from left to right, her toes nudged the gun barrel. She scooped up a pair of damp ankle boots and the gun in one fluid movement. *Game on.*

She spun around so fast she almost gave herself whiplash, aimed and shot the panther in the chest. The boom shattered the deafening stillness in the room. Earthen magic crashed down upon her, pinning her to the floor under a mound of dirt. The crushing weight covered her from neck to feet. It pinned every muscle, and her breath tore at her lungs. She ogled Evan who'd been thrown across the room, his pain-shrouded appearance sweeping her up into familiar pools of icy blue concern. The panther disintegrated, drops of black ink quickly coalescing, then slithering across the room to crawl up Andre's leg. Two more panthers leapt out of the sleeves of the black warlock's custom-tailored blazer, growing as large as Slink. Willow's eyes bulged and she lost air, then sank into oblivion.

Chapter 12

The room suffocated as if Willow lay six feet under, with a peephole to hell. Chanting ensued in a deafening roar. Witches. *Good witches, or bad witches?* A tempest of air, water, fire, and earth magic gyrated wildly in a ring encapsulating Andre and a half-dozen panther familiars.

Willow blinked specks of dirt out of her watery eyes. Someone had blown the mountain of dirt off her, and a fine mantle of mud dirtied her clothes and bare skin. Remaining silent and stationary, she knew better than to interrupt a spell. Not like she wanted to move anyway. Her head pounded and excruciating pain immobilized her left leg. Dirt coated her tongue, and she wiped it off on the inside of her sweater, dredging up moisture and spitting out cat-litter-tasting crud.

Dismayed, she scanned her apartment, one giant cesspool of mud. She found Evan in the opposite corner, not far from where he'd stood prior to Andre's magic knocking her out. Shimmering bands of air encaged his crumpled form in a puddle of mud. Horror clamped on to Willow's heart. Who'd caged him? Was he okay? Should she care? *Oh, right. He filched your magic.* Caring was relative until she got her magic back.

A circle of thirteen Wilde witches guarded by their warlocks intoned the spell to subdue Andre and dampen his magic. Willow suspected their magic was tapped out until they figured out a way to destroy his magic without killing him. Sage would kill to keep him alive. Too much information floated in his head; too much power that could benefit the Wilde Coven, if he cooperated voluntarily—or by force—magical or otherwise. They needed to find out who else was involved in the Black Tide. Evan's information was too suspect at this point. Maybe Andre had something useful to back up Evan's story.

A final synchronized "so mote it be" soared, trailed by thirteen flares of sizzling light. Andre slumped to the floor in his cage of magic. Panther familiars of all sizes fizzled into drops of black ink, and two other witches scooped up the ink into magic-deadening iron containers.

"Willow!" Sage darted out of the circle in the center of Willow's apartment. Sage knelt beside her, cupping Willow's cheeks. "Are you alright?"

Willow spoke haltingly through the crud in her mouth. "My left leg's messed up."

"Your ankle's broken," said Aspen, her middle sister, and coven herbalist. Dabbler in alchemy. Long red hair—redder than Willow's own hair—hid Aspen's face as she formed a wall of impenetrable air around Willow's ankle to keep it stiff and supported. Twenty-eight-year-old Aspen was the one other Wilde witch who possessed air magic. Other than their dead mother.

"Snow found you." Willow touched Sage's palm and her sister drew her hand away as if Willow had cooties. "I knew you'd come."

Sage's face grew stony. "What did that bastard Evan

do to you? He broke my bond."

"He's a black warlock." Willow tried to sit up, and Sage gently pushed her shoulder to keep her down.

"No shit, Sherlock," Aspen blasted out. "Someone needs to kill that lying, betraying black asswipe."

"You rang for my services." Rafael joined them, resting his hand on Sage's head, his fingers combing her ponytail.

The remaining witches and warlocks would keep their magic and focus trained on Andre and Evan until they secured the men in warded cells at the Wilde covenstead in the Santa Cruz hills among the redwoods.

Willow swished her hand through the air. "No You can't kill him. He bound my magic. He's a weaver." Was that the sole reason she wanted him alive? She refused to think about anything else or she'd crumble to pieces and lose herself among the debris covering every inch of her apartment.

"Goddess almighty. It's true." Sage wiped a film of perspiration off her brow. She held out her hand and Rafael hauled her up against him. "If we tapped into the magic they hold, we'd rule the world of witches." She said that as if she knew for certain the black warlocks would fall to her command. "Wouldn't you like that, my love?" She hugged Rafael and pressed her lips to his in a quick kiss.

"Whatever you say." Rafael nipped at her lips. Willow didn't miss the calculating stare icing his eyes. Never one to twist words, he'd always been forthright about wanting to change the ways of modern witches and rule equally with Sage, very similar to what Willow wanted. Sage followed the old-world order to the T. Or did he want to master Sage the way she mastered him? Who the hell knew? She was done with that day and all warlocks. And by the calculating smirk on Sage's face, she was done with all witches. For now.

Sage disentangled from Rafael, standing tall and regal

in her black turtleneck sweater, black leather pants and inky stiletto boots. She may as well have worn a black pointy hat too. "Love, will you carry Willow to the car? The doctor's on standby at the compound."

"Of course." Rafael effortlessly scooped Willow into his muscled arms, cradling her close. She smelled his sandalwood cologne, hating the nasty scent more than she disliked him. He deliberately brushed his hand across her breast.

"Thanks," Willow said for Sage's benefit, barely restraining her frustration of Rafael, hating that she needed assistance. "Knock it off," she mumbled, glaring up at him. He'd always had a hard-on for her, and once had chased after her before Sage set her sights on him, before he'd even hit Sage's radar. She never told her sister about it, didn't want to ruin their tight bond. Even then, he hadn't stopped pressuring her to seek the coven's protection... and sometimes his bed. Had he chased her upon Sage's command to get Willow under the coven's control? No way. Sage would never allow her number one minion to screw anyone else, let alone her sister. Not even to lure Willow into the coven. Or would she? More distrust set up a flea market in her head.

Coven witches and their warlocks shoved Evan and Andre into the warded van in the parking lot. Rafael, Aspen, and Sage followed at a secure distance.

"What will happen to Evan?" Willow asked her sister, her head resting on Rafael's steely arm.

"Once we get the lay of the land," Rafael replied, "I'll kill him. I may torture him for a while. Who knows? Depends on my mood."

"I wasn't talking to you." Willow slugged his arm as he deposited her on the backseat of his big, bad black SUV.

Sage sighed. "Don't freak, Willow. We won't hurt him until he returns your magic and we get answers." Sage's eyes narrowed and her lips kicked up in a knowing smile. "You have feelings for him! Was he as good in the sack as I always imagined?"

Rafael growled louder than the beefy engine of his he-man vehicle.

Willow suffered her sister's I-told-you-so smirk. She massaged her aching temples. "I don't have a clue. He played me. He betrayed me to Charlemagne. He stole my magic. I don't know how much was real, how much fake." *Why won't my brain work?*

"But did he screw your brains out? Worth all his brawn, good looks, and whip-smart mind?"

Rafael glared at Sage's grin and laid his hand possessively on her thigh.

"Maybe," Willow conceded, closing down her brain to Sage's taunting laugh. Part of Willow remained enthralled by the way Evan spoke of defying the way of modern warlocks, and it intrigued her to no end.

Before Rafael had picked her up, Aspen had given Willow an anti-pain potion, but a dull, thumping ache up the length of her leg refused to die. She needed a pain potion top-off. Cringing, she closed her eyes and shut out the world until they arrived at the Wilde mansion on the covenstead grounds.

By the time the coven's doctor on retainer wrapped a fiberglass cast on her broken ankle and Willow's two sisters, cousins, and aunts fussed around her before leaving her in her old childhood bedroom, deep exhaustion bogged Willow down. She wanted to sleep for a week, no dreams, no nightmares, no nothing. Vanquishing the black spell was the one good prize to stem from Evan stealing her magic. "Hooray for small favors," Willow groused into her pillow.

Aspen still hovered in the room, cleaning up the medical debris. Rattling and crinkling noises followed

Willow's epiphany.

She shook her head back, conking it against the headboard of her queen bed. *Oww.* She rubbed her skull, the new pain fighting for dominance against painkillers flooding her bloodstream. *Holy crap!*

"Lie back and sleep," Aspen said, her voice soft and soothing. "Nothing will go down overnight. Everything will be here tomorrow."

Painkillers and a tranquilizer chaser liquefied Willow's body. "Is Sage holding council for her plan of attack?"

"Tomorrow."

"Wake me."

"Coven members only." Aspen grinned, knowing it pissed Willow off that she wasn't invited when she was the main course of the feast.

"The meeting's about me!" In slow motion, she slammed her fist on the bed, her limbs growing languorous.

Aspen intoned a sleeping spell, and Willow drifted off to the land of nothingness.

☪☪☪

Groggy and out of sorts, Willow woke before the seagulls soared into the graying skies of coastal dawn. The absence of her abysmal magic created barren pockets throughout her body that literally ached from the emptiness. She hated that she missed her magic so much when she never had a real chance to exploit it.

Head pain-free, she swung her legs over the edge of the bed and grabbed the crutches leaning against her nightstand. Fortunately, Aspen had cleaned her up and washed her hair before turning her into a pharmaceutical paradise, and she didn't have to fear viewing a crone in the mirror. She carefully slipped on worn yoga pants and a clean, baggy T-shirt she'd found in her dresser.

She had a consuming need to talk to Evan. To see him, kiss him, smell him. Goddess alive, she had it bad for this man who may be dead within the day. She'd never get close to him in the basement cells guarded by a million witches, warlocks, and magical wards. Hobbling to the rear staircase, she contemplated how she'd hop down the stairs.

"Going somewhere?" Rafael's deep, slightly nasally voice arose behind her, berating and amused at once.

"Hit the nail on the head of obviousness."

"Need my help?"

Stunned, she slowly pivoted on her crutches to face him. "You'd help me get downstairs?"

"Willow, no matter what you think, I want what's best for you. Right now, it's Evan. I think he can awaken your magic once he unbinds it. I believe him, even if Sage isn't a hundred percent."

Shock jolted her heart. "What the what? Why?"

"I know the Ravenwoods. Andre led all their witches and warlocks astray. They're good people, with a few exceptions. Evan's tried secretly for several years to convince his family, mainly his eldest brother and family leader, Ethan, to wise up. They'd never have joined the Black Tide if Andre didn't hold something powerful over their heads along with Andre's death threats."

"Did you know Evan had infiltrated the Wilde Coven for the sole purpose to exact Andre's dirty work?"

"No." Rafael moved closer, walked his finger slow and soft across Willow's arm. "In that, we stand united. He tricked us even though his real intent was to turn on Andre."

"Yet, you defend him?" Juggling her crutch under her arm, she swatted his hand away. He leaned forward and kissed her cheek, pressing closer despite Willow's splayed hand on his sinful chest, trying to keep him at a distance. His usual hateful cologne awoke Willow's hormones and fire speared low in her abdomen. For the first time since she'd met him years ago, she witnessed the raw power and magnetism Sage loved about him. His short, layered dark hair, tanned angular cheekbones, and Roman nose over his full pouty lips left Willow confused. How had she never *seen* him? Or seen what Sage recognized, or why all the other single witches constantly worshipped at his feet?

What had Evan awakened in her? Even though she shouldn't, she wanted him more than anything. She wanted everything he'd offered her before he betrayed her last night. A total reversal in her plan of life. *Holy upside-down, alternate universe, Batman!*

"He came around, didn't he?" Easing back, his eyebrows peaked mockingly. A hot storm assailed Willow's neck. "Although he needs to prove himself, *you* made him see the true way. Our way. I was working on him, but you hit a hole in one."

Sage wouldn't exactly break into a happy dance if she knew Willow and Evan held the same goals of equality rather than the good ol' witches-as-dominant-over-the-warlocks standard litany.

"What does Andre hold over the Ravenwoods?"

Rafael shrugged his hands. "One reason we can't kill Andre yet. What's in his head can turn the tide."

"No pun intended?" She turned toward the stairwell again. "Take me to Evan," Willow commanded.

"After council, Sage will force Evan to unbind and return your magic. Until then, stay in your room."

"I command you to take me to him immediately!" Willow stamped her crutches on the stone floor. Her first-ever command to a warlock felt epic, yet missing the exhilaration it should have afforded her as a true member of the coven. Her determination caused her no small sense of joy. One measly night had flipped her life into another twilight zone. She planned to take the night back. She refused to allow a lame limb and lack of magic reduce her to a sniveling nothing.

Rafael bellowed out a throaty laugh. "Girl, you aren't a coven witch. You're not the High Priestess. You don't command me. *You* take orders from me while you're living here."

Willow fumed, holding tight to her crutches to keep herself from bashing them over his fat head.

Cocking her head to the right, her lips curled up in a knowing smile. "What if I *was* a witch of the coven? What if I held more power than any of you?"

She left him standing there bewildered, lines of concern fanning his wide eyes.

Chapter 13

Impatience thrumming through her bruised and battered body, Willow waited for the summons from the coven council. While waiting, she cleaned up and primped despite her gimpy ankle. She donned a black sleeveless sheath she'd found in the depths of her closet stuffed among ten other dresses she hadn't wanted when she'd left her family home. Most of the dresses had tags on them and waited for her to become a real coven member.

The slinky black dress glued to her like a second skin, and she admired the look in the full-length mirror in the bathroom. The dress accentuated every curve to her advantage, enough to make a grown man pounce—based on her prior experience with the horny coven warlocks—with her long auburn hair spilling down her back in ultra-shiny, loose waves. She'd never worn anything other than jeans and T-shirts among the coven, and she felt sexier and more powerful than ever.

No longer the outcast, she had power, albeit slowly emerging magic. That is, before Evan had enslaved and stolen it. *Asshat warlock.* She may not be one hundred percent ready to join the coven, but nothing would stop her from exacting change in their small world of witches. Not after the last couple days and all she'd learned.

"Damnit, Evan. Why'd you have to betray me?" They could've made enchanting magic together. Was it too late?

She rummaged through her dresser and found an old scarlet butterfly pin, a gift from her mother before her familiar came alive. Surprise wound through her, and she missed Crimson flitting across her shoulders in her familiar's typical dance of anticipation. How had her mother known? Admiring the pin tacked to her shoulder, she put on a pair of garnet crystal chandelier earrings.

Wistfully studying her childhood bedroom reflected in the mirror, with the queen bed and scarred white-washed furniture, memories of her parents sank her heart. Painting her room purple and black with her mother had brought more joy than sadness. Her mother had been the High Priestess until a drunk driver ran her parents' car off the road and killed them when Willow was seventeen. Some of the coven's witches believed her parents' demise caused Willow's magic to remain dormant, that the trauma and heartache proved too great for her. Her lack of magic and their death had driven Willow from the covenstead after high school graduation. It had become too painful to live among the familiar shadows. Six years later, the pain had subsided and Willow had grown up a little, despite it. Sleeping in the house for the first time since she'd left almost felt okay. Not normal, but bearable.

The expected summons arrived at ten via Aspen and two older warlocks, Ben and Matthew, both bonded to her two aunts. Maybe Sage didn't trust the younger warlocks around Willow any longer? Both Ben and Matthew gaped at her, and Willow suppressed a giggle.

"Wow, epic cleanup, little sis." Aspen grinned. "I dig this side of you. You might fit in here one of these days."

Sooner than you think.

Crutches in place, Willow hobbled between Ben and Matthew to the council room. They didn't touch or assist her, but sandwiched her between them in case she stumbled. The massive room was crammed to standing room only, and gaping mouths and bulging eyes swiveled toward Willow.

"Willow, you look lovely." Sage smiled and gestured at a cushioned chair next to her seat at the head of the walnut table. Somber shades of gray paint splashed the walls. Willow suppressed a shudder as the creeptastic lifelike eyes on the various portraits of their ancestors seemed to land on her. She could slice the anticipation in the room with a flaming sword. *If Evan hadn't stolen my magic, that is.*

Rafael helped her to the chair and rested her crutches against the sideboard chest to her left. He bent down and whispered in her ear, "You're beautiful. This look suits you." Reverence on display, he kissed the back of her hand. The brush of his lips fueled her she-power, and she deliberately shoved her boobs out to brush against his arm, smirking at his backward jerk. He had to appear the consummate, faithful lover and consort to Sage in public.

Preening inside, she knew how much beauty played a part in their coven. It normally sickened her. Finally, she understood the power it offered. However, it was useless clout as a Wilde witch without magic and brains to back it up. Two out of three wasn't enough.

And without Evan as her warlock. *Shit on a stick.*

Her spine stiffened against the chair as the realization whacked her once again. After toying with the idea of a place in the coven, she'd refuse a position without him at her side, if his betrayal was proven false. They'd make a formidable team to change the tides.

Sage banged her gavel on the wooden block in front of

her. "All to order." The gavel clattered on the tabletop as Sage set it down.

Voices faded until only the sound of rustling clothes and breathing permeated the room.

"Willow. The council has decreed to temporarily release Evan Ravenwood from his bonds in order to prove his fealty to the coven and to return your magic."

A breath Willow didn't know she held wafted out, and another intangible mountainside slid off her shoulders. She nodded acceptance.

"I've reviewed the Book of Dark Magic, and the sole method to transfer, unbind, or release your magic is by the manner *stolen.*"

Willow expected no less, and her eyes hazed over with untimely lust and nerves. Evan may destroy her in more ways than one if they made love again. She gulped. "Okay. Whatever."

"However, we don't trust him enough to allow the two of you alone in a room. A circle of thirteen will surround you, ensuring nothing goes awry."

Willow tried to jump up. Instead, she jammed her left foot against the table leg, shooting red-hot pokers up her leg. Slumped against the chair, she sucked in the pain and gritted out, "You're not serious!"

Sage glowered at her. "It's not your choice. My way, my rules."

Willow slammed her palm on the thick, wooden tabletop, her palm landing on her mother's initials carved onto the surface. "You're not the boss of me, Sage." She drew strength from the memories of her mother ruling at the head of the council table that'd served the Wilde witches for over a hundred years.

Sage leaned over the table toward Willow. "Don't test me, little witch. You've caused enough trouble for us, and we've done *everything* to help you."

"I thought you helped because I'm your sister and you love me," Willow shouted, wishing like mad she could stand. "Didn't I expose a threat to *your* coven, giving you the opportunity to contain it?"

Voices escalated, debating both sides, and the noise in the room swelled.

"Silence," Rafael roared, clanging the gavel down until the room quieted.

"Rafael, help me stand." Willow hated resorting to his aid. He obeyed, his arm around her waist holding her up, his embrace steady and calming. "Do you trust me?" she whispered to him.

"Yes," he replied instantly and unequivocally.

She addressed the room. "Let me do this my way. If I regain my magic and subdue Evan, obtain his fealty, and prove his innocence, I'll join the coven. On my terms." *Game. Set. Match.*

Hollers and whoops charged the room. Stunned, Willow gripped Rafael's hand. She'd had no clue how much the coven wanted her, even without her full magic.

What the what? "What the heck do I offer the coven other than boosting its numbers?" she whispered in Rafael's ear.

"You. Just you," he whispered. "We already know your magic is ripe for the taking. Plus, we'll need a good legal advocate on our side since your father passed. You know how the coven doesn't trust outsiders."

"I'll have rules and wards in place." Sage consented, hiding a smile behind her cold demeanor.

"I expected no less." Willow ducked her head, hiding a smirk.

Sage slammed the gavel on the wood block, the sound echoing up to the twelve-foot ceiling. "All in favor of Willow's terms, say aye!" The assenting roar deafened.

Unanimous vote. Go freaking figure. Pain slicing up

her leg, Willow let Rafael help her sit again. After a soft, fatherly caress on her face, he drifted to Sage's side, her loyal guard dog. Appreciation spilled from his eyes, and he nodded at Willow.

Rafael and Sage had gotten exactly what they'd wanted. Or had they? Satisfied and a little frightened, Willow waited for Sage to clear the room to discuss terms of her joining the coven and protecting her in Evan's company.

After her grueling session with Sage, Aspen and Ben helped Willow to her bedroom to await Evan. Since magic and wards deadened his "dungeon" cell due to Andre in the next cell, they were forced to allow Evan to come to Willow's turf. Sage agreed to a measly hour alone. While Aspen attended to her wounds, Willow attended to her nerves, breathing in and out deep and slow.

A bit of power had shifted to Willow that day, creating a headiness of heart, lightening the burden and guilt she'd experienced since her parents had died. She had no doubt she'd finally live up to her mother's expectations as a Wilde witch after her magic filled her once again and she awakened it her way. Or Evan's way if it worked.

Left alone, Willow freshened up. Biting her inner cheeks, she waited for Evan and a potentially volatile reunion, hence the gaggle of witches and warlocks standing outside her bedroom. *Brilliant.* Like she needed an audio audience.

Sage left her a drawer full of spelled potions, a knife, and a gun to subdue Evan if needed. And a playful butter-soft leather, cat o' nine tails whip from her personal bedroom stash. *Ah, jeez.*

Jittery, she lay on her bed, back against her headboard, ankle resting on a pillow, heart beating a million miles a minute. A knock sounded and the door opened. Two guards roughly propelled Evan inside the room. The door slammed shut behind him, the bang reverberating up the walls. Magic wards ascended, feathering over Willow's skin. Evan wouldn't make it out alive if he tried to leave.

Willow's heart galloped. Her gaze slurped him up from his feet to his free-flowing hair, and she'd never seen a more welcome sight. They'd allowed him to shower, but purple bruises had formed on his jaw and arms, and cuffs had nearly sliced the skin off his wrists. Willow wanted to kiss those bruises and cuts until they disappeared.

Evan rushed to her, his forehead creasing as he tentatively perched on the edge of the bed. "Are you okay?" Hesitantly, he smoothed his hand down her left leg, stopping shy of her cast. Hot tingles chased his touch. And they weren't tingles of the magical kind.

"Hairline fracture."

He gripped his thighs. "What now?" Willow sensed he wanted to pull her into his arms, but fought the compulsion.

"What you said to Andre—"

"Willow, I was playing him to save you. You have to understand that."

"What does Andre hold over your family?" She started with the basics to quell her emotions and hormones from usurping control. He'd refused to talk to Sage or Rafael through several interrogations, indicating he'd only talk to her.

Without a moment's hesitation, as if he knew she'd ask the question, or had practiced his answer, he began, "My family stole the magic from the Charlemagnes during the Witches and Warlocks War, which caused the warlocks to lose the war *they* incited. We spelled them from using magic. Binding spells were woven and the cords were destroyed by witches who basically agreed to a suicide mission."

Her eyebrows rose at this, and he held his hands up in capitulation.

"Happened well before my time." He almost reached out to her, but withdrew when she didn't return the gesture. "Anyway, my ancestors tried to stop the war and correct the imbalance between the witches and warlocks, failing miserably." He brushed his hands over his ripped, clean jeans, seeming relieved to relay his family's deep, dark secret. "After the war, the Charlemagnes planned to kill off the Ravenwoods if they didn't pledge a lifetime fealty to the Charlemagnes and help the warlocks' goal to snag their power back." He winced. "Simple as that. We're slaves to the Charlemagnes, to their leader, Andre. They employed, ruled, or coerced more than enough witch power outside the family to make good on their threat against us. With little choice against the odds, the Ravenwoods fell into line. We've been desperate to find a way out from under his control without his family and allies exacting revenge."

Unpacking his confession, Willow peered at the black tip of Jet's wing peeking out of Evan's neckband. She searched for Crimson, but didn't see her familiar on his exposed skin. "Is the Wilde Coven your way out? Now that we've captured Andre?"

"It's a start. We'll have to deal with the rest of his family and supporters. They'll do anything to retrieve him. Some members of the Black Tide are tired of our dissension and have wanted us out, but feared butting heads if they released us and we escalated into a position of power. Others want out from under the Charlemagne rule completely. But he has plenty of allies."

"Anything as in killing the Wilde Coven to get him back?"

"Yes," he replied. She believed the honesty on his face, playing along the fringes of yearning in his eyes. 'They won't act rashly, though," he continued. "They'll take their time to form a plan, wheedle their way in. They don't typically rush in like fools. But Sage needs to be prepared for anything. At all times."

"Wheedle their way in like you worked your way into Sage's ranks?"

"Yes."

"Will your family pledge fealty to the Wilde Coven?" *Will you pledge fealty to me?*

"Absolutely we can work on an alliance, especially an alliance against Andre and his minions. That's a given. The Ravenwoods know how powerful the Wilde Coven is. This is the chance we've waited for." He extended his hand, withdrew, unsure what to do. "Willow, I'll pledge fealty to Sage. To you. Just let me hold you."

Willow choked down a sob. Nodded. Evan drew her into his arms, careful not to jostle her bum leg. Her body molded to his. Nothing had ever felt so right. Never had she felt so sure of her actions or her belief in him. There didn't appear a smidgen of distrust in his body, his words, or the guilt on his face.

"Before we… before I return your magic, I need to tell you something."

Willow scanned his haggard, handsome face for any other sign that her gut misled her. His concern and sincerity nearly brought her to her figurative knees. She exhaled a sigh of relief. Crimson peeked around Evan's neck and flapped its wings at Willow. Its red wings turned burgundy in mortification, and it rushed behind Evan's neck to hide from Willow's ire. Jet's beady eyes gave her the hairy eyeball, as if the eagle feared she'd vanish if it glanced away. *Weird.* "Lay it on me."

Evan stroked her arm. "When the witches captured Andre's familiars, they didn't capture Slink. It looked like they did. Andre knows how to trick the eye." Willow stiffened against him. "The feline hadn't fully reformed yet and it made her resistant to the drawing spell," he explained. "She's his most powerful coming-of-age familiar."

"Oh, crap on a cracker." Willow hit the intercom button on her bedside phone, an old phone system Sage refused to can for 21st-century technology. "Why didn't you tell Sage?"

"They wouldn't let me see you." His jaw jutted out stubbornly. "I tried to tell Rafael. The fucker refused to listen." He fingered a shadowy bruise on his jaw.

"Get Sage or Rafael," Willow announced into the intercom.

"Then you'll pony up your loyalty," Willow demanded. "Unless you're playing us for fools."

Evan's hand gloved hers. "I haven't led you on yet, have I?" He grinned his wicked, devastating grin that melted Willow from the inside out. "Your command is my wish."

Willow groaned and play-punched his arm. The door opened, emitting her sister and consort. Willow explained the situation.

"Release and waken Willow's magic, Evan," Sage demanded. "Then we take care of this little problem. I want both of you in the dungeon to show your loyalty to the Wilde Coven."

Willow's forehead scrunched. "But my magic won't be up to par. I may not be able to help."

"Aspen told us about your incident in the alley," Rafael threw in. "Evan confirmed it."

Jeez Louise. Did everyone know her secrets? Willow glared at Evan, her glare softening as his gaze warmed and comforted her.

"I want you there, Willow. If nothing more than to watch and learn." Sage half-turned to leave, stopped.

Willow had planned on watching the show anyways.

The idea of helping the coven dominate such a foe cooled her jets sufficiently to maintain her witchy distance. And her broken ankle didn't help much.

"Prove your trustworthiness, Evan, and I may let you live another day," Sage proclaimed. "You'll return Willow's magic, we'll take care of Slink, then you'll arrange a meeting with your family to talk alliance for control over Andre and the Black Tide, to start. Do we have a deal?"

"Hell yes, we have a deal. Trust me when I say, working with the Wilde Coven is first and foremost on the Ravenwoods' agenda. We just needed a safe and secret way in." His gaze landed on Willow, smoldering, sincere.

Willow glared at her sister, as she mentally high-fived Evan. His way in just became her gain.

Chapter 14

Sage and Rafael left, replaced by a cart of lunch from the well-stocked kitchen. In near silent contemplation, Willow and Evan ate a few bites of gourmet sandwiches and sipped wine. Nerves assaulted Willow's stomach and the wine jostled the half turkey sandwich she'd consumed.

"Is it me?" Evan stood and paced to the window across from her. He drew the blinds shut against the afternoon light filtering in from the forest trees outside and potentially prying eyes.

"What do you mean?"

"You're nervous."

"Oh, yeah, right. You bound my magic, stole it, and now I'm supposed to be all hot and bothered that you plan to screw me to return it?"

He turned to face her, winced, scrubbed his hand across the back of his neck. "I can release your magic without... us getting physical."

Willow's head jerked back. "What?"

"But if you want to awaken it quickly, you still need to

be in your deepest vulnerable state." He advanced to her chair and stood mere inches from her. The clean soap scent of him washed over her. "Got any other ideas to get there in our measly hour that's ticking away?"

Willow had already thought long and hard about her conundrum. Nothing had changed from before he'd bound her magic. Not her feelings for him. Only the rules had changed, and he'd veered to the left without thinking. She needed to pull him back to the center.

"Willow, a sense of connection is what gives us a purpose and meaning to our lives. A physical connection like this with magic leads to a deeper emotional and spiritual connection, it opens up your soul to accept the spell. It'll open you up to accept your magic. You've suppressed it far too long."

Time for doing. If nothing else, her magic would lie dormant inside her again. Making love with Evan was a perk. She held out her hand, and he took it, then lifted her in his arms. Evan carried her to the padded window seat and nestled her on his lap.

His butt barely hit the bench when his mouth landed on hers, hard and demanding, then soft and languorous. Air ran in short supply and Willow whimpered. Gasping, he released her and nuzzled her neck, his breath hot against her fevered skin, trailing kisses from her neck to her ear. Magic crackled and Evan created a gentle breeze to cool them off.

He caught her chin in his fingers, forcing their gazes to lock. "Is this what you want?"

"Yes."

"Me or getting your magic back?"

"You. My magic." Willow kissed him. "You, above all." She slanted her head to the side, wiggled suggestively on his lap. "What do you want? Me, *sex*, or my magic?"

"You." He laughed. "And lots of sex."

"Not my magic?" she teased.

"I'd give up my magic for you, the way you make me feel, the way I want you. I don't know what you did to me, little witch. You snared me in your web."

Willow snorted. "You've got that wrong. You *weaved* my magic in *your* web." She pressed her rear on his erection. "And you deserve a spanking. You've been a bad, bad warlock."

"My ass is yours to serve." Evan laughed, a laugh Willow wanted to drown in. He rose, scooping her up again and snuggled her onto her bed, mindful of her lame ankle. He wrapped air around her like soft pillows to support her leg.

In several quick movements, he'd shimmied out of his pants, and pushed Willow's thong to her ankles, quickly unwrapping the dress from her body. Another gust of witch-air pillowed Willow as he moved her closer. He began a dance of desire on her body that incited her unraveling.

With each movement of his body, Evan recited the spell to release and return her magic. A knotted cord of iridescent light whipped in the air above their heads. One by one, the knots untied and the rope of magic crackled like lightning. If Willow hadn't been consumed with the sensations Evan was creating inside her, she would have marveled over his ability to weave magic.

Her unraveling accelerated. "Oh, goddess. Evan. Oh, no, no." She planted kisses on the underside of his jaw.

His spell ended and he grew silent. Earth and air magic pervaded the air in thick shimmers of light. One final shattering thrust into her and they both spiraled out of control.

After several moments and panting, Evan rolled off her to let her experience the return and awakening of her magic and the exquisite sensations it created inside her.

Witch-fire and witch-water bloomed in all the empty

pockets inside Willow. Flames scorched her, and a cooling breeze chased the fiery trails. Fire flickered around them, fanned by billows of air, doused by witch-water before causing damage. Carefully, Willow lifted upright on her knees and swirled her hands above her head. Bolts of electricity flickered off her fingers, and a kaleidoscope of stars sprinkled the room, raining down upon them. Her witch-water misted, keeping the heat from burning them down.

Suddenly, her magic expanded, an airy sensation and a grounding of earth, pinning her to the bed. Water, air, and fire shot off her fingers, drizzled around them. Earth magic kept it centered and controlled. Witch-water misted the bed, and with Evan's earth magic joining it, a red rose grew in the air. Hot, sweet magic connected all four of their elements, connecting *them*. Grinning like mad, she gloried in the magic until it dimmed, and Willow, then Evan, let it go. The flower floated to the foot of the bed, its stems, leaves, and petals disintegrating all over the bedcovers.

Joy and ecstasy left Willow boneless, and she snuggled against Evan's body, his arms holding her where not even his air magic came between them. He rolled them onto their sides, facing each other. She didn't know how she'd foregone such wonder without her magic saturating all the emptiness she'd experienced since her age of majority. And she possessed two elements of magic, more powerful than any witch in the coven other than Sage. *Fire and water! Take that, witches!* Excitement caused her heart to beat double time.

Evan had awakened all her magic, and her trust in him was absolute. And Evan filled the empty pockets of her soul beside her magic, hollows she didn't know were even there.

"Thank you," she whispered. "It worked."

"You were already on the verge." He squeezed her

close. "I feel your magic inside me. It's exquisite."

"Ditto. Your magic is so airy and earthy." She laughed at her play on words.

Myriad butterflies ranging from fly-sized to fist-sized colored the room in rainbow colors. They landed on Willow, her skin absorbing them as tattoos. They roved over and beneath her skin, tickling and itching. Crimson flew up and kissed Willow on the lips before she took her place as her number one familiar above Willow's heart. Rebel, Evan's bonding familiar, settled below Crimson on Willow's left breast, cooing gentle sounds of love as if he'd come home. Her bonding familiar, Rosebud, alighted on Evan's arm.

Joyfully laughing, Willow playfully smacked the flat of her palm on Evan's ass, feeling him quiver and tense beneath her touch. Evan snorted out a sound between a groan and a laugh, sucking in his breath, nearly choking.

"I owed you." She reached behind her and snatched Sage's whip off her nightstand. She trailed the silky leather knots over Evan's thigh, jolting his body against hers. "We might find a use for this later."

"Whoa." Evan grabbed the whip and tossed it across the room. "That's a little too close for comfort. You can *spank* me all you want. But not with that, and as long as you accept my magic."

"Accept *your* magic?" Willow's breath clogged her throat.

"You have my bonding familiar." He touched his finger to Rebel's beak. "And access to all my magic, just like I do of yours." Evan ducked his head in an uncharacteristically shy way. "We complete each other on the spectrum of the four elements."

"Does that mean we're equals, as witch and warlock?" Willow held her breath.

Smoothing tendrils of hair off her face, Evan said, "Yes. Although if you want to dominate me in the bedroom, you'd get no objections. And you can spank me any time I've been bad."

"Do you plan to be bad often?" Willow laughed, free and light, like sunshine bathed her from the inside out. Power waltzed throughout her body, and she felt like she could do anything, wield any witchcraft.

"Very, very bad. Several times a day." Evan's mouth landed on her lips, starting a long, slow kiss. He ended the kiss by nipping on her bottom lip. "Sage won't be thrilled about this. The two of us together can take over the coven. You alone could take over the coven. Four natural elements are better than aether alone."

Willow laughed. "Let's take this one day at a time. I'm not ready for world domination. I'll earn the respect of the coven, as will you. At least, she won't be able to push us around. I'm no longer an outcast and a witch wannabe with untapped magic. And you're not just a black warlock rebel. Sage will never cage you again." Willow tapped a finger on her chin. "Speaking of... how did you use my witch-fire when you had bound it."

A red tide flushed his face. "Um..."

Willow groaned. "Goddess, no more secrets. Tell me!" She pushed against his chest.

"Well, black warlocks can use a little of the magic they capture or bind. Since I wove the spell and captured your magic, there's a residual effect."

Willow hid her face against his chest and groaned. "Tell me you can't bind my magic again."

He shook his head almost violently. "With some exceptions, most witches are still more powerful than black warlocks. *You* are more powerful. Your magic will fight mine and win if I tried to weave another spell against you without your consent."

"Okay. Good. Like I said, one day at a time." She smirked and held back a giggle. "I need to get a handle on my new world."

"Okay. Can we at least go on a first date before our worlds collide?" His happy grin shot silver flecks through his blue eyes.

Willow pretended to think, finger on her lip, brow furrowed.

"Come on!" he barked. "You have my familiar. You know what that means." He tickled her belly lightly, careful of causing her too much movement.

Laughter convulsed Willow. "Okay. Okay. I give. A first date at a nerd convention sounds *nice.*"

"As long as it ends in my bed." Evan stroked his thumb over her bottom lip, shooting tingles to her toes.

"You've got something against my bed? I thought this was an equal partnership."

"Hell, yeah. Your bed's under a foot of mud."

Willow screwed up her lips. "Oh. Right. Guess I'll have to stay here for a while." Jet pecked gently at her arm, and Rebel squawked at the dominant familiar.

She rubbed the preening familiar's tiny head. "Speaking of familiars..."

Rosebud flew off Evan and danced over their heads, not ready to land on Willow alongside the others forming a rainbow of tattoos across her chest, back, and down her arms. Willow commanded the small butterfly to land on her finger. She already recognized its role in her magic, in her life. In Evan's life.

She didn't know what the future held, but a new and exciting path cleared, ending the loneliness she'd embraced to cover up her failings as a witch. For the foreseeable future, she'd begin her new life beside the warlock who'd flipped her world upside down.

"Rosebud, I bequeath you to Evan Ravenwood. With Rosebud, I tie our magic as one. So mote it be." She gently blew on the butterfly, and it landed above Jet over Evan's heart, sinking onto his skin. "So… you wanna be my warlock?"

He laughed. "You witches and your formality. As long as I'm your *only* warlock." Evan kissed her gently, a bare tease across her lips.

She locked her arms around his neck. "One is the perfect number." For the first time in her life, Willow felt whole and complete with everything she didn't know she'd wanted spiraling into her net of magic, the web of her heart.

Chapter 15

E van half-carried Willow down the basement steps. He gently set her standing outside the steel walls to Andre's cell, propped up by her crutches. She fought the strong urge to work her lips up his jaw to his lips, but refrained from the very public display of affection in front of half the coven, in front of Sage who might object with hurtful magic. He smelled fresh of soap and minty shampoo. Willow missed his alluring musky, masculine cologne and planned to rectify the situation as soon as Sage released him.

But business beckoned, and she peeked through the small window on the door. A twin bed, dresser, and a small bathroom decorated the minimalist room. Recessed ceiling lights lit the windowless space. Andre lay stretched out on the bed reading a new, paperback copy of *War and Peace*.

Willow snorted.

Giving Andre no time to assimilate the intrusion, thirteen witches formed a circle in the center of the basement. Starting at the East and working clockwise through South, West, and North, they lit the candles. The usual warlock guardian suspects backed them up. The protective wards around the cell fell, and Rafael unlocked and opened the steel door to the cell. Magic crackled in the air as the coven prepared for any contingency. Protection wards had to be vanquished for their spells to work. A very risky proposition against anyone with magic, let alone a black warlock like Andre. The witches began chanting in a low murmur, their voices undulating up and down.

Sweat beaded on Willow's forehead. Rafael picked her up and carried her to a warded circle. Yelping, Willow beat at his shoulder, and Evan growled at the dominant warlock.

"You shouldn't be here," Rafael whispered-yelled.

"I need to witness. Plus, Sage wants me here. My magic may help. Oh, and by the way, Evan and I are bonded now."

His eyes softened into pools of amber, and he nodded his head in Evan's direction. "You're into him?"

"What if I am? What's it to you, *Dad?*" Willow refused to cage her sarcasm. They kept their voices low for their ears only.

"Sage won't release him to you."

"He already broke their bond. Did you miss the part where I said *we're* bonded?"

"That's not what I meant, Willow. He'll never be yours completely. Sage will keep her hook in him." Willow detected a note of jealousy in his voice.

OMG. Did he worry Sage will want Evan, a strong black warlock? Ousting himself as her top dog? *Am I his backup plan?* "Puh-lease. He's already mine." *Whoa, did I just say that about a warlock?* How her life had flipped upside down in a few days. "Sage won't have a choice in the matter. He's my warlock now."

"In time, maybe," Rafael groused.

"Support me in this, and I'll turn Sage toward you.

Make her give up her other warlock consorts. For good."

Rafael's eyes lifted, glowed as if the sun rose on them.

A steel panel on the wall slid down, giving them a view through an impenetrable glass window, quieting their not-so-light banter. The chanting of the witches swelled as their spell took hold. Evan entered Andre's cell, the remaining magic wards falling with each step he took. Evan's magic vaulted up, so familiar to her. Bands of air—his air magic—enclosed Andre, restricting him from wielding magic. Willow tuned Rafael out, refusing to crack under his pressure and say things she might regret if he kept pushing the matter.

Before anyone batted an eye, a slash of black jetted through the doorway past Evan. Growing larger, Slink prowled, snarling and growling in front of Willow, a paw over the warded protective circle she stood in, then a second paw as the familiar advanced into the circle with Willow.

The wrong circle.

Bigger than ever, the lethal panther menaced. Willow screamed and jumped back, caught in Rafael's arms before her ass kissed the floor. Pain ignited from her ankle to her thigh and she gritted her teeth. She teetered on the edge of the so-called warded circle. It obviously wasn't keeping evil out.

Half the thirteen witches and warlocks surrounded the panther, and Willow backed herself and Rafael out of the circle completely to avoid the magic. Magic crackled and flared as slash after slash of killing lightning blasted ineffectually against the panther, fully protected within the circle. Willow flinched. *Holy flames in hell!* What kind of black magic penetrated a protective circle?

Willow glared inside the cell where Evan held Andre in chokehold straps of air, rimmed in her witch-fire. She whipped her head around to the panther familiar. Magic popped in her core in a silent answer to Evan brandishing her magic. It adrenalized her, ate the pain of her fractured ankle. It felt immensely right. She closed her eyes to concentrate on subduing the panther. The witches and warlocks surrounding the circle holding the panther were getting nowhere. Was Andre the only one who could master his familiar?

A catch-22. If Evan released Andre to incapacitate Slink, Andre may take down the entire room and escape. As it was, the witches of the coven have had to work double time to figure out a way to hold Andre indefinitely in the Wilde covenstead, with wards and spells that wouldn't interfere with the coven's magic. Sage planned to use him as leverage against the black warlocks, but not if Andre managed to kill them all. From what Sage had told her earlier, they'd found an archaic spell to bind his magic. It was simple, stunning and enlightening. First step, getting rid of his damn familiar.

"Clear a path," Evan yelled, fighting his bonds against Andre, his face red and straining. He hauled out the gun Willow had given him from her nightstand. "Get ready to move Willow out of aim." Hands on Willow's hips, Rafael nodded at Evan.

As soon as the crowd cleared away, Evan mouthed, "One, two—"

Slink pounced forward.

Strong hands gripped Willow's hips and Rafael vaulted up and sideways. Slink leaped after them, and the booming gunshot echoed off the walls, vibrated in Willow's eardrums. The panther dissolved, dripping into black ink bubbling on the surface of the glossy cement floor, in the center of the witch's circle drawn to encapsulate it. Candle flames flickered and flared, dancing in a non-existent breeze. Aspen voiced a spell over a jar and coaxed every drop of Slink inside. She capped the jar and triumphantly held it above her head.

Evan's momentary diversion afforded Andre enough time and momentum to dismantle his air shackles and break the magic wards enslaving him. In the blink of an eye, he rose large and substantial in front of Willow, pushing everyone in his path to flounder on the black floor of the basement. Shouts and roars escalated as chaos reigned in the room.

Andre shoved her in the still-warded circle and stood too close in front of her. The other witches couldn't breach the circle, and jumped back as they stepped over the salt lines as if scorched. Air, water, and fire magic created a cyclone of useless magic against Andre. There was only so much magic they could employ without hurting Willow.

Andre's air magic had captured Willow and held her in the circle. She fought the restraints but it was like fighting a steel shroud. The circle was meant to keep magic out, but once inside, all bets were off, apparently. Willow could work with that strange black magic, though.

"Hold your magic," Sage ordered, waving her arms above her head to temper the residual magic in the air.

"Let her go, Andre," Evan commanded. "You'll never get out of this alive."

Andre sneered. "So, Evan, my boy. You've gone to the dark side as they say, eh? Do you understand what your defection will do to your family?"

Evan's eyes hooded over. "Do you know what will happen to you and your minions if you touch Willow?"

"Then I guess we're at an impasse." Andre grinned a Cheshire-cat grin.

Willow's magic rose inside her, fire and water in separate threads, neither dominating the other. Could she work them both at the same time? It was too soon, too much to contemplate. Evan's magic simmered in the mix, but she had no clue how to work air and earth magic. Instead she concentrated on the fire, recreating the sensations and spells she'd produced in the alley the other morning.

"Release Willow and we'll grant you some leniency." Cool and calm, Sage began her negotiations.

Andre uttered a derisive laugh. "We both know you have no plans to grant me any clemency. It was a stroke of the goddess' luck that you captured me in the first place. A momentary weakness I have no plans to repeat."

Embers sparked inside Willow's core. More embers than she remembered from earlier. Evan surreptitiously had moved to the other side of Andre who was now sandwiched between Willow and Evan. She met his gaze, beseeched him, and he nodded at her. He mouthed, "Take control of the fire. You can do it." She remembered that their bond had created a link between them, a nifty side-benefit of bonding a warlock. Damn, she sure needed a crash course on being a witch... now that she was truly one.

"What do you want, Andre?" Sage asked.

"Willow. Nothing new."

"She's been tapped," Evan said.

"A situation that will cost you dearly, Evan," Andre threatened. "But I can work with your leftovers. Once you're dead, she'll be mine to bond. She might not be as pliant as I'd hoped if you hadn't awakened her magic, but I'll make some concessions to endear her to me."

The word "dead" nearly stopped Willow's heart. But she had no time to fall into her fears, and she had to breathe in deeply to quick-start the ticker. As she exhaled, the first tingling of fire finally reached her fingertips. Fire sparked off her hand and the barest shimmery ball began to form. But she feared forming a ball of fire that Andre would see. How the hell was she going to do this? He had one eye on her and the other on Sage. Evan on the other hand was slightly behind him and out of Andre's peripheral vision.

Willow felt a tug and sweep of air magic inside her, or at least that's what she thought it was. An airy sensation cooling the fire and at the same time fanning it to life. Hiding the fire inside her. And then it dawned on her. If she used Evan's air magic to surround her ball of fire, Andre would never see it coming. *Bingo.* She might make a good witch yet.

Willow glanced at Evan, saw him finger the sign for air and fire, and close his eyes while he concentrated on internally weaving a spell.

"What are you doing, witch?" Andre spun on her. "I feel your heat. Don't you dare raise magic against me. I can kill you on the spot."

"It's your death wish, Andre," Sage shouted, her arms flailing in the air, stirring the residual magic to keep Andre from using it.

The witches and warlocks closed in on the circle. Aspen nudged Evan, but he didn't budge a muscle, eyes still closed, weaving his spell to aid Willow.

Air magic rushed into Willow and fanned the flames of her fire. She was burning up from the inside. If she didn't expel the magic, she'd combust. Fireballs formed on both hands held at her sides. They grew to the size of grapefruits, and the air shrouded them, made them invisible except to Willow's witch-eye. Could she toss them at Andre through his shield? Could she toss them without them backfiring onto her? *Holy hell in a handbasket.* It was then she realized that Evan was tearing her shroud apart, bit by bit, air against air.

Andre roared and lunged at Evan, hands groping for his neck. Evan stumbled backward, Andre on top of him, all the while maintaining his destroying magic against Willow's shroud. Several warlocks tried to physically separate the pair, but Andre easily thrust them away with his strong air magic bent on killing Evan.

Air began to soften around Willow, and she mentally and physically pushed through the thin residue. The fire begged to be released inside her. Yet if she attacked Andre, she feared hitting Evan who was still pinned beneath him, both of them in a chokehold.

Evan released his grip on the air magic now that she was free, and she used his magic to strengthen her flaming orbs, no longer caring who saw them. Frustration beat like a caged bird in her chest. Sage's wide eyes and the shock on the faces around her as they stared at her gave her the impetus to act. With a slow toss, she rolled a ball along Andre's backside. Another ball quickly formed on her right hand.

Andre bellowed, his hands losing their grip on Evan's neck. Evan managed to roll Andre off him and jumped up and out of the way.

This time, Willow tossed balls of fire around the black warlock's still body on the cement floor. Air fanned the flames up a foot and encapsulated Andre in a ring of fire. With Evan's help, they quickly erected another shroud of air around Andre and managed to float him into his magic-dampened cell where his body thudded to the floor as the magic dissipated.

Rafael slammed the door shut, the automatic lock clicking into place, and he spun on Willow. Thick walls now muffled Andre's enraged bellows. A trio of witches and six warlocks took up their duties to guard the cell. The spell to bind his magic was already in play and would take a few days for completion.

"Damn, girl, I'd say you're officially a witch now," Rafael said, his pride showing in the bright flecks in his eyes. "Think you can douse the ring of fire before you burn the house down?"

Exhausted, she rolled her eyes at him and sprinkled water off her fingers over the ring of fire. "Are we done here?" She locked eyes with Evan, and her gaze slid to the purpling bruises forming around his neck. "My warlock and I need a break."

In one fluid movement, Evan stood beside Willow, his eyes seeming to hold his touch as his gaze landed on her lips. She wanted Evan's hands on her so bad, she nearly wrapped her arms around him. The terror of the last few seconds sagged her against his accepting embrace, but she clenched her fists to her sides. Unable to take the bold step of touching him, she still reveled in the haven of his wide chest.

"Good work, all of you, in subjugating this situation." Sage approached Willow and Evan. "Well done, Evan. We appreciate the assist, even using our own magic." She nodded at Willow, her eyes glowing with a strange light. Pride and something else. Fear? "And you, my sister. That was a magnificent display of magic for any witch, let alone a new witch. Welcome to the coven. You are truly a Wilde witch now."

Ben handed Sage the discarded gun Evan had brought in. She cast the gun's barrel down Evan's tight arm muscles, glowering at Rafael's jealous growl and caveman stance. He appeared ready to lock Evan in a stranglehold.

Willow studied Rafael and knew she was right. She softened toward him, understanding him and his motives. He'd wanted Sage exclusively all this time, yet being the High Priestess, she had the right to take any warlock, and as many as she wanted who proved fealty to the coven. *Poor Rafael. Although he's her main consort, he may never be number one in her book.*

"Your actions this morning, Evan," Sage continued, "work toward your favor. You're free to return to Willow's chamber. You're free to be her exclusive warlock if she desires. Our bond is broken. I accept it." She stroked her owl bonding familiar on her arm.

Willow hid a smile at her sister's generosity, knowing exactly how she wanted to spend the next few days. If Evan was willing.

"Come, all." Sage gestured to her witches and warlocks. "We have planning to do. I expect quick retaliation from the Charlemagnes."

Willow and Evan returned to her room. She thrust her crutches aside and nearly fell into his open arms, exhaustion and exhilaration bogging her down. The only thing she wanted soothing her battered mind, body, and soul stood with his arms wrapped tight around her.

"You're mine," she said.

"Did you ever doubt it?" He nuzzled her neck, and she exhaled out the ghastly day. Breathing in deeply of Evan's earthy sweat and residual magic, she relished what the future promised her. With Evan by her side, everything was possible.

BLACK WARLOCKS PROWLING

Wilde Witches – Book 2

Read Sage and Rafael's story in *Black Warlocks Prowling*, Wilde Witches – Book 2.

ABOUT THE AUTHOR

After lamenting the lack of young adult books to read, award-winning and *USA Today* best-selling author, Erin Richards, wrote her first novel at the age of eighteen hoping to shift the tide. But the only tide she shifted was moving from high school to college. Then everyday life took its toll on her writerly dreams until she couldn't ignore the writing bug any longer. By then, she had immersed herself in reading adult fantasy and romance novels. Writing suspenseful paranormal and fantasy romance was a no brainer and she went on to publish two adult romance novels and hasn't stopped since. But her muse wanted to give that YA writing gig another chance, and Erin finally realized her lifelong dream of publishing a YA novel with the debut of *Vigilante Nights*.

Erin lives in California. In her spare time, she enjoys reading (of course!) and perpetually landscaping her yards, even though she hates digging holes...unless she's burying fictional bodies! She also confesses to a fascination with American muscle cars... and reality TV shows!

Visit Erin Richards online at:
www.erinrichards.com

Sign-up for her newsletter at:
www.erinrichards.com/connect.htm